"I know w..."
she said quietly.

Hunter sighed heavily. "Oh, God. I'm not quite sure where to start…what to say." He gave her another genuine, heartfelt smile.

The tenderness of his expression hit her right in the heart, but despite her fantasies she recognized she couldn't take that personally. Any kindness Hunter extended was merely courtesy necessary for good communications and a good relationship for Tyler's sake.…

"Tyler's at school right now, but he'll be home about three."

Hunter's brow furrowed. He stared at her. "Excuse me?"

She cleared her throat. "Tyler, our son, is at school right now. But he'll be home about three."

Hunter grabbed Abby's wrist to interrupt her. "Tyler? Our *son?*" he repeated, his face white with shock. "We have a son?"

She wet her dry lips. "Hunter…"

"Abby, do you really believe I would have left you?" He caught her gaze. "That I would have left a child…my son?"

Dear Reader,

This holiday season, as our anniversary year draws to a close, we have much to celebrate. The talented authors who have published—and continue to publish—unforgettable love stories. You, the readers, who have made our twenty-year milestone possible. And this month's very special offerings.

First stop: BACHELOR GULCH, Sandra Steffen's popular ongoing miniseries. They'd shared an amazing night together; now a beguiling stranger was back in his life carrying *Sky's Pride and Joy*. She'd dreamed *Hunter's Vow* would be the marrying kind…until he learned about their child he'd never known existed—don't miss this keeper by Susan Meier! Carolyn Zane's BRUBAKER BRIDES are back! *Montana's Feisty Cowgirl* thought she could pass as just another *male* ranch hand, but Montana wouldn't rest till he knew her secrets…and made this 100% woman completely his!

Donna Clayton's SINGLE DOCTOR DADS return…STAT. *Rachel and the M.D.* were office assistant and employer…so why was she imagining herself this widower's bride and his triplets' mother? Diana Whitney brings her adorable STORK EXPRESS series from Special Edition into Romance with the delightful story of what happens when *Mixing Business…with Baby*. And debut author Belinda Barnes tells the charming tale of a jilted groom who finds himself all dressed up…to deliver a pregnant beauty's baby—don't miss *His Special Delivery!*

Thank you for celebrating our 20th anniversary. In 2001 we'll have even more excitement—the return of ROYALLY WED and Marie Ferrarella's 100th book, to name a couple!

Happy reading!

Mary-Theresa Hussey

Mary-Theresa Hussey
Senior Editor

Please address questions and book requests to:
Silhouette Reader Service
U.S.: 3010 Walden Ave., P.O. Box 1325, Buffalo, NY 14269
Canadian: P.O. Box 609, Fort Erie, Ont. L2A 5X3

Hunter's Vow

SUSAN MEIER

SILHOUETTE *Romance*

Published by Silhouette Books

America's Publisher of Contemporary Romance

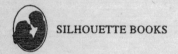

SILHOUETTE BOOKS

ISBN 0-373-19487-0

HUNTER'S VOW

Books by Susan Meier

Silhouette Romance

Stand-in Mom #1022
Temporarily Hers #1109
Wife in Training #1184
Merry Christmas, Daddy #1192
*In Care of the Sheriff #1283
*Guess What? We're Married! #1338
Husband from 9 to 5 #1354
*The Rancher and the Heiress #1374
~The Baby Bequest #1420
~Bringing Up Babies #1427
~Oh, Babies! #1433
His Expectant Neighbor #1468
Hunter's Vow #1487

*Texas Family Ties
~Brewster Baby Boom

Silhouette Desire

Take the Risk #567

SUSAN MEIER

has written category romances for Silhouette Romance
and Silhouette Desire. A full-time writer, Susan has also
been an employee of a major defense contractor, a
columnist for a small newspaper and a division manager
of a charitable organization. But the greatest joy in her
life has always been her children, who constantly
surprise and amaze her. Married for twenty years to her
wonderful, understanding and gorgeous husband,
Michael, Susan cherishes her roles as mother, wife,
sister and friend, believing them to be life's real
treasures. She not only cherishes those roles as gifts, she
tries to convey the beauty and importance of loving
relationships in her books.

Chapter One

Abby Conway had always believed Hunter Wyman would return to Brewster County for her.

Except in her dreams and fantasies, he had been wearing armor and riding a white horse. Handsome, virile, masterful, he would swoop down, securely grasp her wrist and scoop her up, nestling her between his hard chest and the horse's reins. His warmth would enfold her, his strength would protect her.

She never once pictured him standing on the back porch of her bed-and-breakfast, shielding himself from a heavy April downpour with a neat black umbrella. Though she had clearly envisioned his beautiful gray-green eyes and his chiseled features, she never saw an expensive taupe trench coat casually slung over the shoulders of an even more expensive black suit.

And never, ever, in her dreams had she been standing in her kitchen, her red hair haphazardly tied in a knot at the top of her head, her jeans and sweatshirt threadbare and outdated, her nose dotted with flour.

"Hunter," she said weakly because, frankly, that was all she could manage.

He smiled. "Abby." Though almost seven years had passed and volumes and volumes of pain stood between them, his eyes warmed, his smile grew. "It is so damned good to see you."

Abby's eyes misted and her heart thumped. "It's so damned good to see you, too," she said, and swallowed the lump of emotion that tightened her throat.

"May I come in?"

She knew there was no reason to keep him out, yet she glanced around uneasily. Old habit, she supposed. "Sure."

She pushed on the ancient wooden screen door and granted him entry. Careful, polite, he stepped into her green-and-yellow kitchen. Holding the door open, he turned to lean his umbrella against the wall of her porch, then faced her with another broad smile.

"I can't believe I'm really here."

"I can't believe you're really here, either," she said, meaning it. Her mind was working a thousand miles a second, pulling her out of her fantasy and grounding her in truth and reality. If he wanted *her,* he could have come back years ago. Given that he hadn't, she had to force herself to see and understand that he was here only for his son.

Honesty compelled her to admit that if Hunter had come to claim Tyler after leaving her to have their baby by herself, there was a part of her that wanted to rail against him for the suffering of seven long, difficult years. However, there was another part of her that was too cold and tired to fight. In the last four years, the family fortune had been eaten up by medical bills and both of her parents had died. She was alone and broke and needed help, but more than that she was beginning to see that Tyler missed the influence of a man. She could raise him by herself, but Tyler would know life only as a one-dimensional struggle.

So, if Hunter Wyman wanted to be in his son's life, Abby was willing to admit he needed to be there. Pragmatic and poor, she was also willing to concede his return was better late than never.

"I think I know why you're here," she said quietly.

Hunter sighed heavily. "Oh, God, what a relief. I wasn't quite sure where to start...what to say." He gave her another genuine, heartfelt smile. "I should have known better."

The tenderness of his expression hit her right in the heart, but despite her fantasies she recognized she couldn't take that personally. Any kindness Hunter extended to her was merely courtesy necessary for good communications and a good relationship for Tyler's sake.

"Tyler's at school right now, but he'll be home at about three...."

Hunter's brow furrowed. He stared at her. "Excuse me?"

She cleared her throat. "Tyler, our son, is at school right now. But he'll be home at about three."

Hunter grabbed her wrist to interrupt her. "Tyler? Our *son?*" he repeated, his face white with shock. "We have a son?"

She gaped at him. *He couldn't possibly be denying it!* "You knew very well I was pregnant when you left."

"Abby, your parents told me our baby had died."

The blood drained from her face. "What?"

Hunter dropped her arm and ran his hand across his

eyes. "Your parents told me you'd miscarried, Abby. That you didn't want to see me…that you blamed me for losing the baby because I'd upset you… That's why I left town…" He rubbed his fingers over his eyes again. "Oh, dear God."

Oh, dear God was right, Abby thought, falling to one of the chairs around her kitchen table. As if the impact of seeing Hunter after so many years wasn't enough, the realization that her parents could have been so cruel finished the job of buckling her knees. Her parents hadn't liked Hunter, but Abby never thought they'd hated him enough to ruin her life—or to deprive Tyler of a father.

She wet her dry lips. "Hunter…"

"Abby, do you really believe I would have left you?" He turned, caught her gaze. "That I would have left a child…my *son?*"

At eighteen, alone, scared, pregnant, listening to the explanations of two parents she believed loved her, Abby had thought it all made sense. At twenty-five, looking into Hunter's candid eyes, his compelling face, she knew the truth. It hurt so much that her hands began to tremble. "Oh, God."

Hunter drew a long breath. "Okay, let's not panic," he said. "I came here to apologize to you for leaving without saying goodbye and to get your forgiveness so we could both let go of the past. The plan has changed a little bit, but that doesn't mean we can't work this out."

The first half of his words reassured her, the second half didn't sound like Hunter at all. Confused, she surreptitiously peeked at his sedate trench coat, his expensive black suit, the shoes that probably cost more than she'd paid for Tyler's entire school wardrobe, and it suddenly hit her that seven years had passed. Seven winters, springs, summers and falls. Seven Christmases. Seven Thanksgivings.

Though the daydream that got her through many a difficult day had been having Hunter Wyman ride up on a white stallion to take her and Tyler away from all their troubles, the truth of the matter was she didn't really know this man at all.

Worse, he said he had come to get her forgiveness so he could let go of the past—which meant he wanted to let go of her.

He wanted to forget her.

He had as much as come right out and said it.

"Why didn't you tell me about Tyler?" Hunter demanded of his best friend and partner, Grant Brewster, as he paced the floor of Grant's den.

Tall, muscular, black-haired Grant leaned back on the burgundy leather chair behind the huge mahogany desk. Though Norm Brewster had died the year before, the familiar study was still the headquarters for the Brewster fortune and the old chair still the seat of power.

Grant crossed his arms on his massive chest. "How the hell was I supposed to know you didn't know?"

"How *could* I have known?"

"You left town in the middle of the rumors that Abby was pregnant. The whole town knew she was having your baby. I figured you had your reasons for leaving and if you wanted me to know them, you would tell me."

Hunter sighed. "Her parents told me she had miscarried."

Grant conceded that point with a nod.

Hunter sighed wearily. "I should have realized they lied."

"But you didn't," Grant said, sounding old and wise and enough like Norm Brewster that Hunter's head came up sharply. "You might have been twenty-four, but you were fairly immature. Forgive yourself and move on."

"That's approximately what I told Abby we needed to do." Hunter paused, then began to pace again. "I meet Tyler this afternoon. We're not putting it off or hedging the truth."

"Good for you."

When several seconds passed without Hunter making any further comment, Grant prodded, "But…"

"But I'm scared to death."

"Don't be. Tyler's a great kid. Abby's been a fabulous mother. In spite of some very difficult years." Grant shifted on his chair. "If you want the truth, I'd say your return is perfect timing. She needs help."

Hunter turned. "What kind of help?"

"Every kind of help. She's working as a waitress at the diner to supplement her income because the bed-and-breakfast doesn't make that much money, and her parents' illnesses exhausted every cent her family had. She's overworked and underappreciated."

Hunter took his seat in front of Grant's desk. "So, she needs money? I can pay child support…. Hell, I can pay back child support…. I *want* to pay back child support."

Grant caught Hunter's gaze and held it. "You owe more here than child support. If you're going to survive your return to this community, people need to see your integrity. You can't just talk about it. You can't just toss money around."

"Are you saying that in order for our construction company to make the transition from Savannah to Brewster County I have to make amends for my past?"

Grant shrugged. "Only if you want people to respect and trust you."

Knowing Grant had deliberately hit a nerve, Hunter laughed. "You're a dog."

"I'm an honest, forthright dog because that's what my father taught me." Glancing down at the paperwork on his desk, Grant dismissed his partner. "Now, go do the right thing."

"Come in, Hunter," Abby said with a smile, as she held the screen door for him that afternoon. "Tyler's not home from school yet, but that's normal when it rains. Unless I missed my guess, he and his friends are probably jumping in puddles."

Laughing nervously, Hunter stepped inside and shrugged out of his coat. Though it had insulted him that Abby's family had never let him beyond the kitchen, right now being in the kitchen gave him a homey, welcome feeling. A sense of rightness, a sense of comfort.

A sense that he belonged here.

Memories of the love and laughter they had shared all those years ago lured him but Hunter fought them. Thinking this through after his talk with Grant, he had actually considered that to the residents of rural Brewster County, Pennsylvania, "doing the right thing" by Abby meant that he should marry her. He had even considered that if he and Abby could pretend the past seven years hadn't happened, pick up where they left off, and get married, they would be the happiest two people in the world. The picture was so appealing that the temptation to believe nearly dragged him under.

But he also knew the truth about life, people and relationships. There was no such thing as a sure thing. Though he believed Abby had loved him, and he also believed she understood he left because her parents had lied to him, she was only eighteen when they were dating. Not only could her feelings about him have changed as she matured, but she had seven years of hating him under her belt. God only knew what that might have done to her. God only knew how that might have colored the way she had raised their son.

So what he planned to do in his meeting with Tyler, his relationship with Abby, was expect nothing from either of them. He would let them give what they wanted at their own paces, and accept whatever he got as enough.

No expectation, no disappointment. It was a good rule to live by.

However, when Abby turned and smiled at him, Hunter's heart lurched and he once again got the sudden urge to just ask her to marry him and force them into a position where they would have to rekindle their old love. He could still feel the heat and the fire, the passion, of making love to her. It suffused him, seared him with memories he thought long forgotten. Memories that made him ache for the commitment he thought they could have made seven years ago.

However, if circumstances precluded them from attempting marriage then, plain, old-fashioned intelligence precluded it today. Hunter knew so much more about love and matrimony now than he had at twenty-four. And he refused—absolutely refused—to jeopardize his relationship with Tyler because he still had a few flights of fancy about Tyler's mother.

But he had to admit she was beautiful. He had forgotten that. Somehow over the years he convinced himself that she was the red-haired, freckle-faced rich kid who had money but no looks, who had more or less befriended the shy farmer's son because they were both outcasts. Seeing her stunning hair, shot with fire by the afternoon sun, her shimmering green eyes, her smooth alabaster complexion, he remembered things the way they really were. She might not have been popular in high school, but it wasn't because she wasn't attractive. The more he thought about it, the more Hunter realized she had been an outcast by choice. She wanted more, and to Abby *he* had been more.

Her faith in him had puffed him up and boosted him at a critical point in his life. Her confidence literally made him who he was today. And though he couldn't risk a try at the fairy-tale world they dreamed of, he could give her honesty, justice and money. Genuine, hands-on, spendable reality. Not fantasy. If they were going to resolve the problems that faced them, they had to stay away from fantasy and stick with reality.

Glancing around the comfortable kitchen, Hunter recognized that was probably the reason she was keeping them in her kitchen, the room he was accustomed to being in, rather than the living room. This was reality for them. He had to remember that and stay the hell away from daydreaming. He was much too smart for daydreaming anyway. He had gotten over that years ago, and couldn't believe he was slipping back into that bad habit now. He had to be as practical as Abby was.

Right at that moment, Abby wasn't thinking about anything practical, reasonable or even sensible. Not only was she too nervous to be analytical about the finer points of introducing her son to his father, but it hit her full force that she didn't know the silent stranger standing in her kitchen.

She had loved Hunter Wyman all of her adult life, but seeing him again after seven long years, she had to wonder what happened to him. He was as handsome as when he left—maybe more so—but his sedate, businesslike demeanor didn't fit. She couldn't reconcile her Hunter to this composed and quiet man. He had been much too passionate about life to be so...well, stuffy.

"You've certainly changed," she said, wanting him to look at her so she could see his eyes. When her efforts were rewarded by his glance in her direction, Abby's heart sank. He even lost the friendly warmth he had that morning when he first showed up at her door.

"I had to change. I wanted a better life."

She knew that. Part of what drew her to him had been his desire for a better life and the courage and drive she knew would get it for him. "It appears you got everything you wanted."

"And then some," he agreed, taking a seat at the table when she offered it with a wave of her hand.

"Would you like tea?"

He smiled. "You remember."

She acknowledged that with a slight tilt of her head. "I remember a lot of things."

"So do I," Hunter agreed, gazing around the room.

She expected to see at least a shadow of anger, if only because he had hated being banished to her parents' kitchen. But not one iota of sentiment crossed his face. His brow didn't crease. He didn't frown. No memories haunted his eyes. She told herself to be glad that he had grown up and grown beyond his history, but that didn't satisfy the emptiness that seemed to seep into the room by degrees as she came to terms with the new man that he was. He had definitely moved beyond his past, and though she had wished that for Hunter a million times, suddenly she wondered if that wasn't a mistake.

In growing out of his past, he had outgrown her. In moving beyond his roots, he behaved as if he had none.

She handed him his tea. "Here you go," she said, sounding more like a waitress than a friend. She just barely stopped the instinct to reach into her apron for a customer receipt, and the near slip almost made her laugh, but one look at Hunter's serious countenance stopped her. Where was the happy man she'd loved? Where was the smile she had lived for?

"So, you're partners with Grant Brewster now?"

He nodded. "Grant actually saved my construction company. I had hit a rough spot, and he had come to Savannah looking for a place to invest some money. We were a match made in heaven."

Watching him while he talked, Abby was struck by the emotion in his voice. The first real emotion she had heard since his warm hello that morning. He loved his company, but she couldn't help but remember a time when he thought *they* were the match made in heaven. Now he used the phrase to describe a business.

"That's…interesting," she said, then grimaced because her tone conveyed exactly the opposite meaning of what she intended.

Hunter chuckled. "The truth is, Abby, I'm probably not very interesting. I more or less became successful by changing. I'm not wild and rebellious anymore. Not hot-tempered anymore. I don't lose my cool. I handle things."

"That's good," Abby said but she was oddly disappointed. Not that she wanted him losing his temper, particularly around Tyler, but she couldn't stop herself from wondering how this remote stranger could enjoy the prosperity that had once been so important to him.

Forced into a strained silence, Abby peeked at him and the very act of looking at him took her breath away. His dark, dark hair accented the smooth angles and planes of a face that would have made him the perfect candidate for modeling. He was still so damned sexy and gorgeous, it was impossible not to think of him as the guy she had loved all those years ago. Recognizing this really was Hunter—Hunter Wyman in her kitchen!—shot an unexpected ripple of tingles down her spine, which she quickly squelched. This might have been the boy who had wanted to wrap up the world and give it to her gift-boxed, but the man he had become had new beliefs….

Before she could complete her thought, Tyler burst into the kitchen. "Hi, Mom!" he said and immediately reached for a cookie.

With the moment of truth at hand, Abby froze. She glanced at Hunter and saw that he, too, seemed paralyzed. Reserved, composed, he sat motionless, waiting for her to do what had to be done.

She cleared her throat. Gazing at her dark-haired,

grayish-green-eyed little boy, the picture of Hunter in elementary school, she was swamped by fear. It was a good thing—a very good thing—for Tyler to meet his father, but she suddenly had the feeling they could have timed it all a little better. At the very least, they could have prepared him.

However, now that the wheels were turning, it was too late to stop, too late to try to think of a way to make this easier. Hunter was in her kitchen. Tyler was staring at him with wide-eyed curiosity. The ball was in her court.

She stooped to her son's level. When she put her hands on his small shoulders, he gave all his attention to her. "Honey, this man is Hunter Wyman."

As if in slow motion, Abby's little boy lifted his gaze away from her up to Hunter. Instead of seeing the explosion of happiness she expected to see on her son's face, Abby found herself looking at gray-green eyes full of fire.

"Hunter is your father," Abby added slowly.

Tyler's lips thinned and his chin lifted. Because Abby knew her son so well, she easily recognized the look that expressed the bottom line to everything he felt.

Condemnation.

"I know. You told me Hunter Wyman was my father."

"Well, this is him," Abby said brightly. "He's moving back to Brewster County because he's partners with Grant Brewster. So now he really gets to be your dad."

Though he spoke directly to his mother, Tyler never took his gaze from Hunter's face. "He didn't want to be my dad before this?"

"He was away," Abby began, but Hunter interrupted her.

Hunkering down to Tyler's level as Abby had, Hunter captured Tyler's attention. "I didn't know you existed. I'm sorry. I'm very, very sorry," he said honestly, humbly. "Sometimes adults do things that don't make a whole heck of a lot of sense, and people who shouldn't get hurt do." He paused, giving Tyler time to digest that. "I shouldn't have left town without finding out for sure what had happened to you…and your mother." He glanced at Abby for emphasis. "Because I didn't, we didn't get a chance to know each other. This is my fault. I will fix it."

"How?" Tyler asked simply.

Yeah, how? Abby echoed in her head.

Calm, cool, collected, Hunter said, "I don't know yet. But if we take this one step at a time, everything will work out. For right now, though," he said as he rose and walked back to the table, "it's enough to finally get to meet you. If you want to go up to your room or go outside with your friends, I understand." He paused and smiled. "You can do whatever you normally do."

Tyler peered at his mother. "Can I go outside?"

"I'd rather you changed into play clothes first," Abby said, feeling ridiculous making the inane request, given that she had just introduced her son to the father he had never met.

Tyler nodded and raced from the room. Abby turned and gaped at Hunter. "Well, that was warm and fuzzy."

"We're boys, Abby, not girls."

"You didn't even hug him!"

"He didn't want me to hug him," Hunter replied.

"Hell, he didn't even want me to touch him." From the quiver in his voice Abby might have believed that bothered Hunter, but his next words were again detached and indifferent, making her think she had imagined the emotion. "It was almost as if somebody might have told him things about me that made him afraid of me."

Abby gasped incredulously. "What?"

Hunter faced her. "Did you hate me so much that you had to poison his mind against me?"

Abby might have actually appreciated his accusation, if he had said it with some feeling. Since it was delivered with complete composure, she didn't trust it.

"First, I didn't hate you," Abby quietly replied, so confused she knew she didn't dare lose her temper for fear she had misinterpreted something and would make a worse mess out of this situation than it already was. "Second, I didn't tell him anything but good things about you."

"That's not how it looks to me. There's no other explanation for how he could hate me even without knowing me...."

Before Hunter could say anything else, Tyler slid into the room again. "You hurt my mom," he said simply, his chin raised defiantly.

"I didn't mean to hurt your mom," Hunter quickly retorted. But Tyler didn't listen. He grabbed another cookie and shot out of the back door.

"You still expect me to believe you didn't say anything to him?"

Abby only stared at Hunter. She understood that Tyler's jumping in and out of the room—and the conversation—was only his way of dealing with his anger, and typical behavior for a six-year-old. But she couldn't get herself to explain that to Hunter because his insinuation was infuriating. And personal. All these years of sacrifice and struggle, she had never once said anything hurtful or hateful about Hunter. She couldn't stand here and let him make the accusation as if he had the right—as if he had every right in the world to everything he wanted after deserting them.

"Do you really think me capable of trying to get him to hate you? And if I did, why?" she demanded. "To what end?"

"Your parents got rid of me seven years ago by lying to me," he said. "What was their reason for that? To what end?" he asked, mimicking her, but he shook his head as if to stop himself. "Okay, let's just calm down."

Again he hauled back his anger and controlled himself, but Abby's eyes narrowed. She would have welcomed the opportunity to argue any of this out with him, but because she believed it was better not to fight, she reined in her temper just as he had. However, the part of her that was hurt and upset, the part that had been abandoned, knew they would never resolve any of this without an opportunity to clear the air, because they both had feelings they had to deal with. Though Hunter kept leading them in the direction of a real, honest discussion, as if he understood that, too, he never let them finish. Seven years ago he not only would have let her have her say, he would have encouraged it.

And he would have had his say, too.

"The bottom line is that I want a relationship with my son," Hunter said, removing his coat from the back of the kitchen chair. "So if I can't form a decent connection with Tyler while he's in your custody, I'll file for custody myself.''

Without another word he strode out of the kitchen and Abby stood, openmouthed, staring at her back door. Now where had that come from? After the great pains he took to make sure they didn't argue, it didn't make any sense to threaten to file for custody.

For a few seconds, she considered that he might not care to get his say or to hear hers, because he was simply going to push until he got what he wanted— to bulldoze his way into their lives. But she honestly hadn't seen signs of his being unreasonable in either of their conversations. Actually, she hadn't seen signs that he wanted anything at all until his parting shot.

The truth was she had absolutely no idea what to think. She didn't have a clue who he was or how to deal with him. She didn't know how to keep the peace with him, resolve the past, or even come to a halfway decent agreement, because any time an emotion entered the picture, he quickly quashed it.

But one thing was clear. He'd changed. He'd *really* changed.

And she wanted her fantasy back.

Chapter Two

Since Abby knew less was more with her son, she said very little about Hunter that night or on the walk to school the next morning, except to reinforce that Hunter was basically a nice guy who had missed out on being part of their lives. She told Tyler she genuinely believed Hunter would have been there for them if he had known of Tyler's existence. She didn't lay blame on her parents. She couldn't. She didn't want Tyler to hate the only family he had known because of a mistake.

And for her own sanity, Abby had to believe it was a mistake. She had to believe her parents never would have tricked Hunter out of town if they had realized how very desperately she'd loved him and how very much he'd loved her.

Thinking about how much Hunter had loved her, walking from Tyler's school to the diner, Abby smiled. He had been wonderful. Funny. Effervescent. Handsome. And passionate. Incredibly passionate! He had loved life and refused to be beaten by a horrible childhood. He'd intended to be something...someone. And he'd promised to take her with him.

That had been the plan. Lying naked in the back seat of his old car, cuddling after making love, he would tell her his dreams and the very resonance of his voice could convince her he was right. He would have it all. *They* would have it all—together.

She almost couldn't equate the withdrawn stranger with the extraordinary man who had loved life, who had seen the future as bright and beautiful in spite of his humble, disheartening beginnings, and who couldn't wait to make love to her.

Even as Abby served breakfast to the residents of Brewster at the diner, she kept thinking about the way Hunter made love to her. The memories, replete with feelings and sensations, haunted her. The pictures in her mind were so vivid and so complete, she was abundantly grateful for the distraction when the wives of all three Brewster brothers entered the restaurant, each carrying a toddler triplet.

Both little girls, Taylor and Annie, wore pink dresses with ruffle-rump tights and Cody wore a navy one-piece romper that looked like a sailor suit. The babies, now over a year old, got a refill of milk in their "sippy" cups and each woman ordered toast.

Though they tried to make it look as if they'd decided to bring the kids into town for a treat, Abby knew they'd come in to hear about her meeting with Hunter. Evan's wife, Claire, a stunning brunette, was the only one of the women Abby had actually known since childhood. But Kristen, Grant's wife, and Lily, Chas's wife, had become close to Abby in a very short time. When the Brewster brothers became guardians

of their father's triplets, Evan met Claire and married
her. Lily was hired to be the triplets' nanny and Chas
fell in love with and married her. Then when Kristen,
the triplets' aunt, came to Pennsylvania to try for custody of her nieces and nephew, she and Grant fell in
love. Now all three Brewsters were married. Each of
them had responsibility for one of the triplets and
Abby had three friends. She decided not to spare the
details of her meeting with Hunter. Lord knew the
truth always got out eventually.

"He said what?" Lily asked, her big blue eyes wide
and round with confusion. A breathtaking blonde with
a sharp mind for details, Lily was the most sensitive
of the three.

"He threatened to file for custody."

Though Abby didn't want to admit it, and though
she didn't want to see it come down to a battle between husbands and wives, she was glad that the
Brewster women considered her a part of their clique.
Because she didn't know how to handle Hunter, it was
a comfort of sorts to have an "in" with the other
people in his life. If she couldn't get him to listen to
reason, maybe the Brewsters could.

Glancing from Claire to Lily to Kristen Devereaux
Brewster, Abby sighed and wondered about the fair-
ness of using them. In the end, she chose not to. "I
probably shouldn't be talking with you guys about
this." Her gaze drifted over to Kristen, the green-eyed
blonde who was also the aunt of the triplets, babies
who had been in the custody of the Brewster brothers
since the death of their father and Kristen's sister, the
babies' parents. "Especially you," she said to Kristen.
"After all, your husband is Hunter's partner. I

wouldn't want to say anything to cause trouble or hard feelings.''

"Well, you just hush up, now," Kristen said, her Texas accent obvious in the hills of central Pennsylvania. "Hunter may be Grant's partner, but you're *my* friend. And where I come from friends take care of friends.''

"Thanks, but I don't think anybody can take care of this.''

Claire frowned. "Frankly, I don't see what the problem is. For seven years you've been waiting for Hunter to ride back into town and take you away from all this,'' she said, waving her hand to indicate the aging diner. Cody, the triplet for whom she and Evan took responsibility, patted her cheeks as she spoke. "If you ask me, everything will be fine after a few weeks of the two of you getting reacquainted.''

Abby shook her head. "Reacquainted" didn't quite fit the bill of what was happening between them. While Abby remembered a bright, wonderful man full of promise, the Hunter Wyman who had returned was quiet and brooding. And bossy. They couldn't even have a reasonable discussion about Tyler. Getting "reacquainted" was completely out of the picture. "I don't think so,'' she said.

"Why?" Claire demanded. "Has he suddenly grown a second nose?''

"No," Abby said, heat suffusing her when she brought up Hunter's image in her mind. His looks were the very last of his problems. If anything, age had made him even more gorgeous. "He hasn't lost one ounce of his attractiveness.''

"Oh, look at you," Lily said with a laugh. "You're blushing.''

"She's always adored Hunter Wyman," Claire told Lily as if speaking a confidence, but she didn't bother to lower her voice. "He was the older man in her life. The rebel."

Both Lily and Kristen sighed with delight, but the observation made Abby frown. "Maybe that's it."

"What?" Kristen asked.

"Maybe I don't like him because he's not a rebel anymore."

Claire gave her friend a confused look. "You don't like him because he's not a borderline criminal?"

"No, that's not quite it." Abby pulled her lower lip between her teeth as she tried to draw her conclusion. "I think I don't know how to *deal* with him because he's not a rebel. Seven years ago, if Hunter would have decided he wanted Tyler, he probably would have kidnapped him."

All three of the women gasped. Abby shook her head furiously. "I wouldn't have let it happen," she insisted. "But the point is, back then I knew how to handle Hunter. I knew him so well I could have kept him from doing something rash and foolish. I don't have a clue how to handle the man he is now."

"I still say you're worrying over nothing. This is a chance for you to reunite with your one true love," Claire said dreamily. "So, things aren't going exactly as planned. Give it a chance. It will all work out."

"My one true love was passionate and wonderful," Abby said dully. "This guy isn't. This Hunter might be handsome and sexy, but the passion is gone. In some ways he behaves as if he thinks passion is wrong. Or as if he believes passion is the 'bad' trait that held him down in Brewster County."

"Or," Kristen proposed, "because Grant is the passionate partner, maybe Hunter thinks he's the one who has to be in control. Maybe all he needs is a little time or a little push to loosen up.''

"So what are you going to do?" Lily asked.

"I have no choice but to let Hunter see Tyler," Abby said. "He's coming over tonight after dinner."

"Maybe you should try to be a little seductive and refresh his memory about what you shared," Claire suggested, waggling her eyebrows.

Abby blushed furiously. "Not on your life." She might have done that under other circumstances, but she was afraid to now. For all she knew, this Hunter might scold her if she flirted with him.

"What was it you loved about him, sugar?" Kristen asked suddenly.

Though anybody reading her thoughts of the morning would have said the way he made love to her, Abby knew that wasn't true. "He was honest," she admitted quietly, because in her life there had not been enough honesty. Poor as Hunter had been, lonely as he had been, he didn't know any way to behave but with honesty and simplicity. Being with him, loving him, was the easiest thing Abby had ever done. "And direct and genuine."

"Okay," Claire said, sounding relieved. "Those things don't change. Now if you had said his looks, we'd all think you were crazy because looks can fade. But honesty doesn't fade. Neither does forthrightness. He's still the same guy, Abby. You only need to bring out the best in him."

Just the thought that he was the same man filled Abby with yearning. Not simply sexual, but emotional. In that second, she realized how much she missed him, but more than that she understood that she had never stopped loving him. If there was a chance, even a teeny, tiny chance, she could bring out the simple, honest man in him again, Abby knew she had to try.

Dressing that evening, after rushing Tyler through dinner, Abby also reprimanded herself for being impatient. She couldn't believe she had jumped to the conclusion that Hunter had drastically changed merely on the basis of two short meetings. Good Lord, seven years had passed. Many, many things stood between them. Of course, he wouldn't act like her best friend the first time he saw her after a long separation. And he certainly wouldn't behave like a lover.

Confident, composed, Abby jogged down the steps when she heard the front doorbell ring. Though she hadn't exactly dressed up, she hadn't worn jeans and a T-shirt, either, as was her usual practice. Instead, she had exchanged the jeans for a short, flared skirt and the T-shirt for a soft mint-green sleeveless sweater. She wasn't a woman who believed in high heels, but she did have chunky-heeled mahogany sandals that more or less suited the outfit.

Reminding herself that her friends were right and she shouldn't judge Hunter too harshly or too quickly, Abby pasted on a smile and opened her front door. When she saw him, her jaw fell.

He wore charcoal gray slacks and a black turtleneck sweater that not only made him look wealthy and sophisticated, but also made her short skirt and sandals seem totally inappropriate. She felt poor and humble and something like the beleaguered heroine of *Cinderella,* instead of the lonely, ivory-tower princess she used to be.

"Hello, Hunter," she said gaily, though inside she was dying. "I'm afraid I'm a little behind schedule, and I haven't had a chance to dress yet," she said, adding the lie because she refused to be in the submissive position with him again. Surely she had something in her closet that could give his charcoal gray slacks a run for their money. "So, I'll just run upstairs and—"

He caught her hand and kept her from turning to the steps. "You look fine," he said quietly, then almost groaned. Had he said "fine"? She looked wonderful. Cute. Happy. Sexy. Incredibly sexy. "There's no need to change on my account."

"I know," she said, and yanked her hand out of his grasp. Too late, he realized he'd been holding it forever, as if her hand belonged in his. "But you're so dressed up," she added plaintively.

Hunter laughed. "These are comfortable clothes for me now," he said and moved into her foyer, hoping she would relax and follow him. He hated the fact that he made her nervous. The more nervous she became, the more he wanted to console her. And that was bad, even dangerous.

Not only had Hunter heard from Grant that Abby never spoke harshly of him, but he also realized that the Abby he loved wasn't capable of being vindictive, which meant she hadn't said anything but good things about him to Tyler. In one short day every suspicion he had about her had been mitigated or completely resolved by someone, and he kept getting this surge of nearly overpowering emotion that seemed to demand that he ask her to marry him.

Aside from his own miserable marriage failure, he couldn't dredge up one good reason not to marry her, except that seven years had passed and Abby might not want to marry him. Which was actually the clincher that kept him from making a darned fool of himself. Unless he harnessed all the instincts that continually sneaked up on him, he might blurt a marriage proposal. And he could not let that happen. Particularly since he had decided that moving into the bed-and-breakfast would be the best way for him to get to know his son and for him and Abby to have time to hash out their problems. If they were going to live under the same roof, he had to control himself.

"Well, they sure don't look comfortable to me," Abby insisted, her gaze roaming up and down his body.

Hunter felt an instant, instinctive reaction, which didn't amaze him as much as it overwhelmed him. No matter how much his logical thoughts kept reminding him to cool off and settle down, his instincts were screaming that this was *his woman*. He didn't need to cool off or calm down. She was *his*.

Looking at her the same way she'd just appraised him, he couldn't suppress a burst of jealousy thinking she dressed this cute, this *sexy* for her guests all the time. And if she did, why?

But if she didn't, why tonight?

"So, where's Tyler?" he asked, setting his suitcase on the floor beside him and turning his attention away from her and onto the proper matter at hand, before his curiosity and his unwarranted jealousy got the better of him.

She shrugged, then glanced around questioningly. "I don't know," she said, sounding truly confused.

She looked adorable standing in the center of her dark wood foyer. Her bright hair sparkled from a recent shampoo. Her gorgeous legs were exposed beneath the short skirt. Her face was scrunched in confusion. She was nervous and flustered and simply irresistibly dressed, and before Hunter could stop the natural conclusion from forming, it formed. Adding the nervousness and her sexy little outfit together, Hunter couldn't help but think that she might still have feelings for him.

If she had dressed this way specially for him because she found him as attractive as he found her, maybe there was more than attraction between them….Maybe she had actual feelings for him?

Immediately on the heels of that, he realized that he still had feelings for her. Lots of them. Attraction. Desire. And the need to be a parent with her. They had a relationship that resulted in the creation of a child and he wanted to raise that child with her. *With* her. Because she was good, kind and genuine and he knew their personalities complemented each other. He would never be so foolhardy as to think he still loved her after a seven-year separation, particularly since he had been through an ugly divorce and didn't believe love of the poetic, romantic kind existed. But all things considered, if he were to try again with another woman, Abby would be that woman. She was sweet, she was sexy and she had his son.

As all those thoughts rolled to their obvious completion, and Hunter acknowledged that sexual attraction was not the only thing he felt for Abby, he wondered if the impulse he had tagged instinct wasn't actually good, sound logic.

"You know what, Abby?" he said suddenly, breaking the uncomfortable silence. "This is starting to make sense to me."

"This?" she asked breathlessly, confirming what he

had been thinking all along. She did find him as attractive as he found her.

"Well," he said slowly, his logical conclusions urging him on. He refused to be guided by uncontrollable impulses, but sound reasoning couldn't be ignored. Because it was sensible, it had to be right. "I don't want to be forward, but it looks like you probably dressed up for me."

She gasped, but he held up his hand to stop her from commenting. "And I still think you're the sexiest woman on the face of the earth. Adding our attraction to the fact that we have a son, the very best thing for everyone involved would be for us to marry and raise Tyler together."

Abby was speechless, flabbergasted and embarrassed—mostly because he'd guessed she had dressed up for him because she *was* attracted to him. She considered that he was teasing, or didn't fully understand what he was saying because he said it so calmly, so efficiently. But then, for the first time since he'd entered her foyer, she noticed the suitcases at his side.

"What's this?"

"I decided that the quickest way to get to know Tyler would be to stay here—in the bed-and-breakfast." He paused and caught her gaze.

Their eyes locked, and Abby swallowed hard as a hundred possibilities assaulted her. Hunter Wyman would be staying in her home. The man she adored. The man she hadn't been able to resist since she was eighteen. The man she had pined for the past seven years. The man who had just asked her to marry him.

"I hadn't intended to stay for free," he advised pragmatically. "I'll be a paying guest."

His straightforward announcement left her even

more flabbergasted than she had been at his proposal, and Abby stared at him. Where were the sensitive bones that used to be in that wonderful body? Not only was he rolling into her world like a bulldozer on one of his construction sites, but he offered his proposal like a waffle cone without ice cream. It held so much promise, so much potential, but there was no love behind it. She *wanted* to feel the wonderful, heavenly hope that someday he could love her. Instead, she felt only emptiness.

It seemed she was nothing more to him than a hotel proprietor, who just happened to be raising his child.

Where was *her* Hunter?

At a complete loss for what to say, Abby took the only route available to her. She couldn't afford to refuse a paying customer and his staying at the bed-and-breakfast was better than having him file for custody. So she checked him in, gave him a key, and left the room. Tyler hadn't come down to meet with his dad yet, but he would eventually and Abby decided that since Hunter was so good at figuring things out, he would figure out what to do with Tyler when he arrived.

Hunter was baffled, too. Since he only said what was so very obvious, he couldn't believe he'd made her mad. Her leaving angry didn't make sense.

His mind a jumble of confusion, he sat down on the sofa to wait for Tyler but almost before his backside hit the seat he heard, "My mom likes flowers."

Startled, he looked behind him and there sat Tyler, scrunched between the back of the couch and thick velour drapes that enveloped him in darkness.

"Get out of there," Hunter said gruffly, grabbing Tyler's hand and pulling him a little farther out in the open so he could see more of him than the light of his pale eyes. "What the heck are you doing anyway?"

The little boy crawled out from behind the couch. On all fours in front of Hunter, he raised his gaze and said, "I been hiding."

"All this time?" Hunter asked curiously.

Tyler nodded.

The absurdity of it made Hunter laugh. While he and Abby looked for Tyler, he was right under their noses. "Hiding, huh?"

Tyler said, "Yeah. You know," he added, shifting his legs until he was sitting instead of kneeling, though Hunter sensed he'd done it more as a way to avert his attention, than to make himself more comfortable. "Other girls get flowers," he said, his focus skewered on a ball he gripped like a lifeline. "Lily got flowers the one time she stayed at the bed-and-breakfast. Chas brought them." He looked at Hunter. "But my mother never gets flowers. She told Lily she would like some flowers, too."

In a peculiar sort of way, Hunter knew exactly what Tyler was saying. He had walked into Abby's life unannounced and turned her whole world upside down. It was no wonder she behaved irrationally.

"You know, Tyler," he said, rising from the sofa, "I think you're right." Not only would taking Tyler's advice start to form a bond between himself and his son, but it also wouldn't hurt to get on Abby's good side. Because he'd been trying to manage a bunch of uncontrollable instincts by presenting a logical, rational case, he'd just asked a woman to marry him, but he'd done it as if he were proposing a business deal, instead of marriage.

The kid had a point.

Abby deserved flowers.

"Let's go," he said and began to lead Tyler to the door. But remembering Abby's frame of mind when she left the foyer, Hunter thought the better of it, and said, "Go tell your mom you're leaving with me."

Believing Tyler would walk into the kitchen, Hunter's brows rose when the little boy only ran to the door and shouted, "Mom, me and Hunter's going out."

Hunter didn't for one minute consider that appropriate notice, but when Abby called, "All right," as if she were glad to be rid of them, he frowned. Nothing in this household went the way he thought it should.

On the front porch, he turned to Tyler. "Are you sure this is okay?"

Tyler nodded. "Yeah, you made her mad. She's probably in the kitchen trying to bake something."

"Bake something?"

Tyler shrugged and added mournfully, "Yeah, probably coffee cake, and we're going to have to eat it for breakfast or she'll get mad again."

Hunter laughed out loud at the observation until it struck him that he and his son were having a normal, honest conversation. About Abby. Their common bond. Though he might have thought his marriage proposal abrupt, and Abby might have downright hated it, Hunter truly believed he was on the right track.

And Abby would come around.

Given that Brewster hadn't changed much in seven years, Hunter wasn't surprised to find that the Petersons still owned the florist shop. He was even less surprised to find them resting on their back porch in the fading rays of the sun.

"Evening," he said to the old couple who rocked

back and forth on a swing that hung from hooks in their porch ceiling. "Lovely night."

"Great night," old man Peterson agreed. "You new around here?"

Hunter shook his head. "No, I'm Hunter Wyman. My dad and I owned the old place on Church Road. I'm Grant Brewster's business partner now."

"Well, I'll be," Matilda Peterson said, her crochet needle stopping mid-stitch. "Hunter Wyman. Will miracles never cease."

"Yes, ma'am," Hunter said, though he wasn't exactly sure what she meant by that. Was it a miracle he'd done so well for himself, or a miracle he was home? "I'm sure you know my son, Tyler," he added, first, to include the boy and, second, to head off any speculation. Brewster was a small enough town that everyone surely knew about Abby's child. But more than that, Hunter didn't want any question about his plans. Not only was it important that his intentions were clear to everyone, but it was more important for Tyler's sake that the boy understood he had not been abandoned—and neither had Abby.

"I'm here because I need some flowers. You wouldn't happen to be able to open your shop to take my order to have flowers delivered to Abby tomorrow at the diner?"

"Don't need to open the shop," old man Peterson said. "Still got a mind like a steel trap," he said, pointing at his temple. "I'll remember. What do you want to send?"

He looked down at Tyler. "Any idea what your mom likes?"

Pleased to have been consulted, Tyler grinned. "Chas bought Lily roses."

Mrs. Peterson gasped. "Filled the room," she said with an appreciative sigh. "Those Brewsters know how to treat a woman."

"I don't doubt it," Hunter agreed, realizing his friends had a penchant for the extravagant, flashy gestures that typically swept a woman off her feet. Unfortunately, since Hunter knew he had already tossed enough surprises Abby's way by his proposal, he also knew it wouldn't be wise to go overboard with this.

"I think I'll just stick with a dozen."

"Red?" Mrs. Peterson asked speculatively.

Hunter considered that. He knew that the color of a rose you sent to a woman meant something. He could also see from the look of anticipation on Mrs. Peterson's face that red meant something really good.

"Make them red," Hunter decided. "You can bill me or I can stop by tomorrow afternoon and pay for them, but I want to make sure she gets them first thing in the morning."

"You got it," Mr. Peterson said.

Hunter grabbed Tyler's hand and turned to go, but Tyler tugged twice to stop him. "My mom's gonna like the flowers," he said with authority, and Hunter felt pride swell up in him like nothing he'd ever felt before. He wasn't sure if it was the knowledge that he'd pleased his son or the knowledge that he was about to please Abby, but something filled him with warmth and rightness…maybe a combination of both.

"I think you're right," Hunter told Tyler, then a thought struck him and he stooped down and caught his son's gaze. For the first time since he'd met Tyler, Hunter noticed that the little boy's eyes were exactly the same color as his eyes. His nose was the same.

His lips had the odd little upward curl at the corners that was the mark of all Wyman men.

Hunter was hit by a strong, almost uncontrollable urge to hug Tyler. To hold him. To feel the little boy that he'd created. To give him love. All kinds of love. To let him know that he was loved. So loved that Hunter could barely breathe for the strength of it.

But that wasn't appropriate. He didn't really know this little boy and Tyler certainly didn't know him. He didn't want to scare him.

Instead, he steadied his hands on Tyler's shoulders. "One of the most important things about flowers," he said, studying his son's eyes, feeling things that threatened to overpower him, "is that they need to be a surprise."

"A surprise?"

"Yeah, women love surprises."

Tyler's eyes widened comically. "My mom will love a surprise!"

"Okay," Hunter said, again overcome with love for this child who so adored his mother. "Then that makes this our secret."

"Our secret!" Tyler agreed, obviously tickled to be in on something covert.

Quiet, studying each other, they simply stayed on the sidewalk. Hunter waited patiently while the little boy appraised him, but when Tyler blinked rapidly as if becoming uncomfortable, Hunter rose and, with his hand on Tyler's shoulder, began leading him home.

Tyler, however, reached up and took Hunter's hand off his shoulder. Just when Hunter expected him to drop it, he rearranged his small hand inside Hunter's much larger one so that they were holding hands as they walked toward the bed-and-breakfast.

Emotion swamped Hunter again, but he didn't say anything—he barely breathed. He had the sudden, intense feeling that the way to win this little boy's heart was to win his mother's. And though Hunter was absolutely positive he had had Abby Conway's heart at one time, all the rules had changed. Even the playing field was different.

Before they took the first step up the stairs to the front porch of the bed-and-breakfast, Hunter stopped Tyler again. "Now remember," he whispered, "the flowers are our little secret."

Tyler grinned naughtily. "I remember."

In that second, Hunter prayed, really prayed, that the flowers would work. Because he suspected that the same gesture that could win his son's heart, could also lose it if Abby thought the flowers too personal or out of line, considering that this time tomorrow the whole town would know Hunter had returned to Brewster and had sent Abby flowers....

Red ones.

One dozen long-stemmed *red*—for passion, he suddenly remembered—roses.

God, she was going to kill him.

If a private marriage proposal could make her mad enough to leave the room, long-stemmed red roses seen by the entire town would probably turn her into a nuclear warhead.

He had a feeling he was going to be eating coffee cake for days.

Chapter Three

Just as Tyler had predicted, an off-center, slightly burned coffee cake awaited them the next morning.

"I usually get breakfast pastries from the diner for paying guests," Abby said apologetically as she served Hunter a slice. "But I thought it over last night and came to the conclusion that it would be better for Tyler if we didn't treat you as a paying guest." She caught his gaze. "But more like family."

Stranded in the regret of her beautiful green eyes, Hunter didn't know whether to laugh or cry. For Tyler's sake, he agreed with her. It was better to treat him like family rather than a guest.

But something else, something like a need to cheer *her* on also made him feel accepting her decision was the right thing to do. After all, how hard could it be to eat a piece of slightly burned breakfast cake?

"I think it's a great idea," Hunter said enthusiastically. "This looks...wonderful."

He took a bite and chewed thoughtfully, hoping to

get a burst of cinnamon or sugar—or just plain flavor that would give him an honest reason to compliment her. Unfortunately, the burst of flavor never came and neither did the sense that he had chewed enough that he could swallow. Finally, in desperation, he took a drink of coffee.

"That dry, huh?"

"It's coffee cake, Abby," Hunter said brightly. "You're supposed to sip coffee while you eat it."

"Oh, right," Abby said. "I hadn't thought of that."

"Okay, then," Hunter said. He had never seen the shy, insecure side of Abby before and though it was unusual, it was also endearing. All their time together she had been the one with the confidence who spurred him on. Now it seemed fate was giving him the chance to return the favor. Without hesitation or grimace, he took another bite from his cake.

"Morning, Mom," Tyler said as he ran into the room. "Hey, Hunter," he added, jumping onto the chair beside Hunter. Then he saw the coffee cake. "Aw, Mom!"

"Now, Tyler, it can't be that bad," Abby returned, slicing off a piece for her son. "See, Hunter's eating it."

Hunter would have passed Tyler an apologetic smile, but for Abby's sake and since he had a plan to rescue his son, he kept his eyes forward and said, "I'll walk Tyler to school this morning."

"That's all right," Abby said, turning around to face the counter behind her. "It's on my way to the diner."

"But he wants to go in early today," Hunter said, while he gave Tyler a quick look he hoped would convey to his son that he should just go along. "And

I told him I would walk him in. In fact,'' he added, inspiration striking, "he may not have time to finish that cake.''

Abby sighed. "All right. I'll wrap it up for him. He can take it with him.''

"Good idea,'' Hunter said, and when Abby turned away again he caught Tyler's gaze and winked at him. "What time do you go in to work?'' he asked Abby casually.

"Nine or so,'' she replied, her back to Tyler and Hunter. "I don't have to go in until the second wave of the breakfast crowd.''

"That's good,'' Hunter said, then mouthed to Tyler that they would grab a takeout order of toast on the way to school. Grinning foolishly, Tyler nodded.

When Abby turned to hand Tyler his cake, both the men in her life were as quiet and unassuming as church mice, but Abby couldn't shake the feeling that something wasn't quite right. First, Tyler was never this quiet. Second, he now nearly adored the man he had absolutely hated yesterday.

Yeah, she was sure of it. Something had happened.

She considered the possibilities the entire time she straightened the kitchen and dressed in her waitress uniform. She thought about it walking to the diner. She was still thinking about it as the Brewster women entered with the triplets.

"He ate my coffee cake,'' she said without preamble as the women took seats at the counter and Abby poured them coffee.

"I told you he still loved you,'' Claire said, holding Cody back from the hot cup.

"No, I think it had something more to do with Tyler.''

"Tyler?" Kristen echoed curiously. "What the heck would eating *your* ungodly dry coffee cake have to do with Tyler?"

"I'm not sure," Abby said, honest enough about her own cooking that she didn't take offense. "But this morning, when Tyler came into the kitchen he said, 'Morning, Mom... Hey, Hunter.'"

Kristen, Claire and Lily only stared at her.

"He didn't just say hello. He used that friendly, buddy kind of hello men say to each other. 'Hey, Hunter,'" she explained, looking at the three women as if they were slow and dull for not keeping up.

"And this is bad because..." Lily prodded.

"Because yesterday Tyler *hated* Hunter. Almost despised him. I didn't think I would ever get him to speak civilly with the man, then Hunter took him out for a walk last night and now he's acting like Hunter's his best friend."

"Abby, all this is good stuff," Claire reminded her, patting her hand.

"I know that," Abby said, frustrated. "But I just can't help but think there's a reason."

In that precise second, Thadd Peterson, grandson of the Petersons who owned the florist shop, strode into the diner with a long, white box haphazardly strewn across his arm. As if he were a third grader instead of a sophomore in college, he stared at the instruction card, trying to decipher it.

"I think this says Abby Witness," he said to Abby, handing her the card to get her assistance. "I don't know an Abby Witness."

Lily yanked the card from his hands before Abby could take it. "It says 'Abby *Waitress...*' then the next line is, 'At the diner.'"

"Oh," Thadd said, passing the box to Abby. "Here you go, then."

Abby stared at the box. Claire fished into her purse and pulled out a dollar. "For your trouble," she told Thadd, dismissing him. He looked at the money, grinned and walked away. Claire turned to Abby. "Open it!"

"I'm afraid to."

"Well, I'm not," Kristen said, grabbing the box and tugging open the wide red ribbon. Lily lifted the lid and Claire pushed back the white tissue paper.

"Oh," all three said in unison.

Abby looked down at the contents of the box. Long-stemmed red roses. "Oh," she said, too.

"Card," Lily announced, holding out the small white envelope to Abby.

"I'm too nervous," Abby said, backing away.

"Well, it's inappropriate for any of us to read it," Kristen protested, but Claire yanked the card from Lily's hand.

"I've been her best friend since grade school, so it's not inappropriate for me to read anything belonging to her," she said, ripping open the small envelope. "Just what I expected," she proudly announced. "They're from Hunter."

"Does the card say 'Love' Hunter?" Kristen asked.

Claire shook her head. "Just 'Hunter.' But it also doesn't say 'your friend, Hunter,' or 'all my best, Hunter,' or 'I hope we can work things out, Hunter.' It just says 'Hunter' because he expects you to understand. See?" She held up the card for everyone's inspection, then, beaming, handed it to Abby. "I told you he still loves you."

Too confused and amazed to say anything, Abby

only stared at the card. Her first thought was that Hunter still loved her and had truly meant his marriage proposal from the night before. Then she remembered what he had said and *how* he had said it, and that thought disintegrated like snowflakes on warm pavement.

"Well, I think they're darlin'," Kristen said, peeking into the long white box.

"I think they're more like a hint," Lily said, touching the rim of one of the velvety petals.

"You mean a hint that he still has feelings for me?" Abby asked cynically.

"No," Lily said with a laugh. "A hint that the man's soul is still full of passion and romance."

"I agree," Claire seconded.

"Me, too," Kristen agreed, then she leaned her elbow on the counter and sighed dreamily. "So when do you see him again?"

"Tonight," Abby absently replied. Though she couldn't explain the roses, from Hunter's clipped, quick, overly logical marriage proposal the night before she knew for sure she wasn't dealing with a heart and soul romantic.

"Tonight!" Lily gasped.

Abby waved a hand in dismissal. "Don't make such a big deal out of that," she said, reaching for a vase beneath the long red ceramic counter top. "Since he's now living at the bed-and-breakfast—"

"He's living with you!" Kristen sounded elated.

"At the bed-and-breakfast," Abby said, but all three of the Brewster wives laughed with glee.

"That's wonderful!" Claire said.

"Why?" Abby asked, then slipped around the corner into the kitchen to fill the vase with water. Through the rectangular opening that looked out on the diner, she added, "He changed his lodging because he wants the opportunity to get to know Tyler better."

"Yeah, right," Lily said, laughing.

Abby began putting the roses in the vase. "You guys are making too much out of this," she insisted, abundantly glad she was so preoccupied with Hunter eating her dry, lifeless coffee cake that she hadn't told them about his marriage proposal. Because of the way Hunter had suggested they marry and because he hadn't mentioned his proposal that morning at breakfast, she was sure he hadn't meant it for any purpose other than to bring them together for Tyler's sake. In fact, if she looked at these flowers from Hunter's skewed, purely logical point of view, this gesture might actually be an apology of sorts for embarrassing her.

But Lily, Claire and Kristen didn't say anything, only rose to leave the diner as if they were content with the situation and could move on.

"Get with the program," Claire said when she paid her bill. "This guy still has feelings for you. And if you don't start acting like you're at least interested, you're going to lose out."

Abby desperately wanted to believe that. And studying Claire's confident face, that wanting nearly did her in. No matter how calm, cool and composed she appeared, she *wanted* to think Hunter sent those flowers because he was passionately in love with her. That was something the old Hunter would have done. But all she had to do was remind herself of his tone of voice when he asked her to marry him and that bubble of hope self-destructed.

She was very glad she hadn't fallen victim to the

optimistic joy of the Brewster women when Hunter returned home from work that night. He was tired, grouchy and didn't look at all like a man who was "passionately" glad to see her or who was anxiously awaiting her reaction to getting flowers. He looked so *unlike* a man expecting a reaction to a dozen roses that Abby seriously wondered if Thadd Peterson hadn't made a mistake. After all, he had stumbled over reading the card.

"Hard day?" she asked, when Hunter dropped his briefcase to the sofa and plopped down beside it.

"Grueling," he replied then closed his eyes as if sitting were pure ecstasy.

Looking at her exhausted former lover, Abby had to fight off the urge to touch him. She wanted to smooth away the lines and wrinkles of a difficult day's work and rejuvenate him. She wanted to thank him for the roses with a soft kiss. But because he was behaving like a man who had forgotten he had sent her roses, she merely said, "I made a pork roast."

His eyes fluttered open. "What happened to the rest of the coffee cake?"

She grimaced. "It ended up in the trash. I think there's something wrong with my oven," she added as she began to walk to the kitchen, Hunter behind her. Unless he admitted he had sent her those roses, getting rid of the coffee cake was the closest thing to a thank-you she could give him. "Almost everything I bake burns or ends up dry, so I threw it out."

To her surprise, and despite his tiredness, Hunter invited himself into the dinner preparations. Distracted by calculating the ways she could punish Thadd Peterson for putting her in this awkward position, since she was now convinced Hunter had not sent those flowers, Abby hardly noticed how well she and Hunter worked together. But once she settled on an appropriate torture for Thadd, she did note that Hunter was an excellent cook. He seemed to spice by instinct and taste, rather than recipe, and though that was what she did, the aromas coming from his pots were far more enticing than anything she'd ever created.

When Tyler entered a half hour later, their meal was almost ready. Though she expected Tyler to be jumping for joy with the news that they weren't eating her cooking tonight, he didn't say anything, only gave Hunter several odd looks. Abby felt confused, and again suspected something wasn't quite right. She told him to wash up for dinner and he ran out of the room as he normally would. But when he was still quiet through their meal, Abby knew something was terribly wrong.

"What's up?" she asked, then ruffled his hair as she passed him when she returned from getting the chocolate cake she had bought for dessert.

Tyler said nothing.

"You okay?" Hunter asked Tyler, taking the cake from Abby's hands and setting it on the table in front of him.

He gave Hunter another odd look, then glanced at Abby and back at Hunter again. Abby saw Hunter shake his head slightly as if warning Tyler off something, but because they said nothing, she didn't have a clue what was going on between the two of them. Abby despaired that Tyler had gone back to disliking his father, and racked her brain for something to say. Tyler had already given a lackluster report of his day at school and Hunter had provided a brief rundown of his activities, so her options were officially exhausted.

Finally Hunter cleared his throat and said, "What about you, Abby? How was your day?"

It had been so long since anyone sincerely asked about her day that for a few seconds Abby wasn't quite sure how to respond. Then she remembered the roses. Color bloomed in her cheeks. The moment of truth. If he had intended them for her, this would be a good moment. If he hadn't, both of them were about to be embarrassed mightily.

"Actually, something unexpected happened today. I got a dozen lovely roses." She paused and licked her suddenly dry lips. "From Hunter."

Hunter didn't get a chance to react before Tyler asked excitedly, "Did you like them?"

Seeing her son so happy, Abby forgot about being embarrassed. Instead her heart melted. She knew Tyler recognized that she didn't get gifts or special attention, and she also knew this bothered his poor six-year-old heart.

"I loved them," she said, swallowing the lump in her throat, feeling for the first time the true effect of Hunter Wyman in their lives. Hunter could give things to Tyler, do things for Tyler that Abby couldn't. Including be nice to his mother. Because Tyler saw that she went without and that her life was difficult, having Hunter do anything nice for Abby would please him.

"I'm done," Tyler said, then jumped from his chair, ran to her and hugged her. "I'm going outside to play with Billy."

He bounded toward the door but Abby stopped him. "Hey, don't forget you have homework," she said as he slapped the swinging door to the kitchen to open it.

"I'll be back in time to do it," he said and the door

swished closed behind him, leaving her and Hunter alone in the echoing silence that followed in his wake.

"Did you really like the flowers?" he asked quietly.

She nodded. "Very much," she said and busied herself with her dessert because now that she knew he really had sent them to her she found herself wanting to kiss him again. And she was afraid to kiss him. Part of her was afraid that if she kissed him, she would never stop. The other part was afraid that if she kissed him she would be reminded yet again that he was a different man from the man who had loved her seven years ago.

She didn't need to be reminded of that. All she had to do was look at his clothes, the way he carried himself, and she knew he wasn't the same man who had fathered her child.

As if to prove that, and furthering Abby's theory that sending those roses didn't have the grand meaning for Hunter that everyone thought it did, he dropped the subject of the flowers. They ate their dessert making small talk and then Abby showed Hunter an office at the back of the downstairs where he could do some of the work he brought home with him. He didn't come out until around nine and when he did he found Abby and Tyler finishing his math at the kitchen table.

"I'm sorry, I probably should have been here for this," he said, sounding miserable, running his hand across the back of his neck.

"It only takes one parent to do homework," Abby assured him.

"You can help me tomorrow," Tyler suggested, as he shoved his papers into his book and then shoved the book into his backpack.

"Okay, that sounds like a good deal," Hunter

agreed, obviously liking the idea. "I'll help every other night."

Abby immediately recognized another benefit of Hunter's return home. She would get some assistance. She could see herself having time on her hands. Though that was a good thing, curiosity about how Hunter and Tyler had forged this sudden friendship of theirs tiptoed across her brain again.

She would have suspected the flowers had something to do with it, but Tyler's good feelings for Hunter arrived before the flowers had. She knew Hunter hadn't bribed him the night before. They weren't gone long enough to have seen a movie or even to get ice cream.

Completely at a loss, she considered that maybe she was making too big of a deal out of nothing, but it was just so unusual for Tyler to do a complete turnaround in his feelings for someone. Especially overnight.

"You wanna come up and help me get ready for bed?" Tyler said to Hunter, and Abby's mouth fell open, even as every suspicion she had multiplied by at least three.

"Yeah," Hunter agreed with a grin. "That's a good idea." He and Tyler left the kitchen without another word.

When Hunter returned downstairs and announced that Tyler was in bed and had been read a story, Abby concealed her continued shock at the depth of this new relationship and went upstairs to say good-night to her little boy.

Tucking the covers under his chin, she said, "You seem to like Hunter a little more than you did before."

He nodded.

"As fathers go," she said, groping for words to get him to open up and not really thinking of anything inspired, "you could have done a lot worse."

"Yeah, he's all right."

"Anything you want to tell me?" she ventured uncertainly. "Anything I should know? Anything that bothers you?"

He shook his head. "No."

"Well, if you do remember something that bugs you, something that you don't understand or don't like, you know you can tell me, right?"

He nodded again. This time he added a little smile.

Her eyes narrowed. It just wasn't like Tyler to instantly adapt to someone like this. Worse, unless she got an explanation for this behavior, she would worry that her little boy was becoming too trusting.

Knowing she couldn't question Tyler anymore without upsetting him, Abby went in search of Hunter and found him on her back porch swing.

"Hey," he said, as she pushed open the screen door. "Have a seat," he offered, patting the cushion beside him.

Cautiously, she did as he asked and then forced herself to relax because she didn't want to look like an idiot if Hunter and Tyler's good feelings were genuine. After all, Hunter was Tyler's father and it was a good thing for Tyler to adapt to him so quickly. Abby had known he was more than ready for a man's influence in his life, so this was good.

Good.

Everything that was happening was good.

Biting back a sigh, Abby realized what was troubling her. Everything happening was good, so she was waiting for the other shoe to drop. Because too many difficult things had happened since Hunter went away, it was hard for her to settle herself and accept anything good.

Like the fact that he was here. Hunter Wyman, the man she had always loved, was here. He'd sent her flowers, he loved their son, and now they were alone.

Maybe he was her Prince Charming after all?

"So, what did you do to Tyler last night to get him to trust you?" she asked simply, without animosity, like one friend talking to another. Even if he was her Prince Charming, she still wanted this mystery solved.

Luckily, Hunter laughed. "We had a guy talk. Very important to us and nothing for you to be anxious about."

"But I am anxious," she answered honestly. "I'm concerned that accepting you so quickly will have him lowering his natural defenses around strangers."

Hunter only looked at her. "Has anyone ever told you you're a worrywart?"

She shrugged. "I'm a mother. Worrying is part of my job."

"Well, relax," Hunter said, then casually draped his arm across the back of the swing and behind her. "There are two of us to handle the job now."

She tried not to jump to conclusions about why his arm was six inches away from her, by focusing on how relieved she felt to have someone with whom to share parental responsibilities. Unfortunately, that didn't work. Heat seemed to radiate from his skin and flow to her neck, reminding her that she was sitting on her back porch with a man who theoretically had his arm around her.

So she switched to telling herself that she didn't have anything to fear because this was Hunter. But just thinking that sent a tingle of emotion down her spine. She loved Hunter. Always had. Probably always would on some level. And now here they were. Alone.

Concentrating on breathing, she forced herself to calm down and said, "I certainly don't mind having help with the child care responsibilities, but more than that I recognize Tyler needs a man's influence in his life."

"I agree," Hunter said casually, as the arm he'd laid across the swing shifted downward and landed on her shoulders.

Abby's chest tightened. "There are lots of things he needs to learn," she said, trying to sound as composed as he was. "Like fishing."

"Fishing," Hunter said in such a way that Abby knew the idea appealed to him. "That'll be great. I love to fish. And it's a great way to bond."

"Yes, it is," Abby agreed, but just when her comfort level had gotten to a safe place again, Hunter's hold tightened. He cupped his hand on her shoulder and his fingers began kneading.

Abby officially stopped breathing. Not because his touch was arousing—although it was—but because she didn't know what was going on. For all practical intents and purposes, the arm across her shoulders could simply be a friendly gesture. They were talking in a casual, cordial way, and their topic of conversation was basic life details they needed to handle. He could intend his arm across her shoulders as nothing but companionable. And Abby could be misinterpreting everything.

Or he could be making a pass at her.

Just the thought shot pleasure through her—which was exactly why she had to be careful. If he wasn't making a pass at her, she could very likely say or do something foolish.

"It's a beautiful night," Hunter said, shifting her closer to him, nestling her against his side.

Shivery tingles ran down her arms and most of her muscles went numb. He was definitely making a pass at her. And she was definitely enjoying it. She had missed this man for seven years. She thought about him every long lonely night. She had his child. And now he was here and he was definitely making a pass at her.

Not precisely sure of what to do, but absolutely positive being involved with Hunter was what she wanted, if it was what *he* wanted, Abby looked up at him. He glanced down, and for several seconds they only stared at each other, then he lowered his head and kissed her.

For Abby, the whole world exploded with stars. Seven years of frustration and loneliness disappeared. Every hope she'd ever had got a new breath of life. Just from one soft press of his lips to hers.

She tentatively slid her hands on his shoulders and shock waves of happiness ricocheted through her. She greedily memorized every sensation of having her hands on him and having his arms around her, and before she understood what was happening, she found herself tumbling headfirst into a kiss that had gone from simple and chaste to openmouthed and passionate in about ten seconds.

She was so hungry for the taste of him that when he parted her lips with his tongue, she granted him entry. She wanted to savor every sensation and greedily, hungrily kissed him back. When they finally broke apart, both of them were breathing heavily.

"If that doesn't prove we're made for each other,"

Hunter said, holding her close, "I don't know what does."

Abby couldn't have agreed more, and could barely keep herself from shouting with joy. She had waited seven years for this man, for this love, and now she was the luckiest woman in the world.

"That's why I don't think it's wrong that we marry for Tyler's sake. The offer from yesterday still stands."

At first what he said didn't penetrate Abby's passion-hazed musings, but when it did, disappointment cooled her ardor so quickly she felt as if she'd fallen off a cliff and landed on a rocky shore.

And suddenly the flowers made sense.

She pushed out of his arms. "Do you really think you can convince me to marry you with a few flowers and some kisses?" she asked incredulously.

"I don't see why not," Hunter said casually, calmly. "We have more going for us than most engaged couples have. We share memories and a history. We have a son…and we have a great passion for each other."

Though Abby was momentarily buoyed by the mention of their great passion, she saw that he thought more of their memories and history, and their son, than he did of their passion. She swallowed the indignation that rose in her, along with the disappointment. Why? Because she set herself up for this by being fanciful. A son was a very important bond for a man and a woman, and it was logical for Hunter to think more of Tyler than anything else at this point. And since they hadn't seen each other in seven years, all they had were memories and history.

Though she wished he would stop talking marriage,

he wasn't wrong. *She* was wrong. She kept trying to build her relationship with him into something it wasn't. Something it would never be again.

Rising from the swing, she blew her breath out and finally took the logical, realistic, un-fairy-tale-like course of action that she should have taken yesterday by saying, "We really don't know each other anymore and I'm not marrying somebody I don't know."

Weary, tired, she left the porch.

Hunter bit back a curse. Everything had been perfect. Moonlight. Roses. Good dinner. Help with Tyler. Sharing. Communication. They had it all. But in the last second something had gone wrong.

He couldn't believe it.

As weary as Abby, Hunter went in, locked the kitchen door and made his way through the downstairs, turning off lights on his way to bed. Climbing the steps, he dejectedly went though the events of the evening in his head again. He couldn't understand why Abby would be so stubborn when everything seemed so obvious to him.

Because he was lost in thought he almost tripped and fell when Tyler grabbed his arm and gave a solid tug that yanked him inside his bedroom.

Standing on the oval braided rug and dressed in pajamas covered in trucks and bulldozers, Tyler said, "I heard what you said to my mom about getting married."

Positive Tyler was either confused or angry, Hunter's first instinct was to panic. He fully expected to be yelled at since Tyler didn't like anybody hurting Abby, so he was surprised when Tyler added, "How can you marry her, when you've never taken her on a date?"

Knowing this required tact and diplomacy, Hunter lowered himself to Tyler's level and said, "Your mother and I knew each other before. We went on plenty of dates."

Tyler shook his head. "Everybody gets dates but my mom. Claire had dates with Evan. Lily had dates. My mom doesn't get to go on dates."

"That's because..." Hunter began, thinking he needed to explain this situation to Tyler one more time, but suddenly what Tyler was innocently saying made perfect sense to Hunter and he smiled.

"You know what, Tyler?" he said, then rocked back on his heels. "You're right again."

"I know," Tyler said, sounding older and wiser than his six years, and though Hunter got the strongest urge to hug his sensitive child, he rose and directed the little boy back to his bed.

"You just go to sleep," he said, tucking Tyler under the covers. "And I'll take care of everything."

"You're going to take her on a date?" Tyler insisted.

Hunter nodded. "As soon as I can arrange it."

Tyler sighed with relief. "Okay," he said then closed his eyes and rolled over on his pillow.

Overwhelmed with love for the little boy who loved his mother so much, Hunter tiptoed from his room.

But in the hall another thought struck him. All this time Hunter had been thinking so logically about everything, he forgot that getting married to Abby could affect Tyler in some ways that might not be positive. Given that this particular little boy was bright and perceptive, would it be good for him to see two people marry only because they were his parents?

Or would Abby and Hunter somehow be setting a bad example that could possibly hurt Tyler?

Chapter Four

While shaving the next morning, Hunter seriously weighed the pros and cons of everything that would happen if he and Abby married, and he concluded that ultimately Tyler would benefit more than lose. So he decided to take his son's advice and ask Abby out on a date, but he waited until Tyler finished his breakfast and ran to his room to get his backpack before he made his suggestion to Abby.

"I was thinking that maybe you and I should go out on a date tonight."

Standing by the kitchen counter, wrist deep in flour because she was baking, Abby froze.

"Last night you said that our problem was that we really don't know each other anymore," he explained, "and I realized that could be why I keep insulting you when I don't mean to."

For that, she turned and looked at him, and he continued.

"I'd say it's also why you keep getting angry with

me. After seven years of being apart, we don't even know each other well enough to have a decent discussion. So the logical thing to do is to go on a date."

Though he expected her to argue, she cleared her throat and softly asked, "Where would we go on this date?"

He shrugged. "A movie is always a good place to start. We could have dinner together at the diner first."

Abby didn't know whether or not she agreed that going on a date was a logical way to get to know each other. But, studying the handsome man in front of her, a man who was trying very hard to integrate himself into his son's life without causing too much tension, a man she had wanted back in her life for seven years, Abby decided she had to try one more time. Hunter was right. Their problem truly was that they didn't know each other. A few hours of honest conversation and camaraderie might cure him of accidentally insulting her and cure her of jumping to conclusions. And who knew? With a little time and effort, maybe they really could have the relationship they both seemed to want.

"All right."

"Since we both have work in the morning, we'll go to the seven o'clock movie," he suggested, and Abby nodded but that was the end of the conversation because Tyler came bounding into the room.

As far as Abby was concerned, it was better to keep their romantic complications out of Hunter's relationship with Tyler, so she said nothing, except goodbye when Hunter ushered Tyler out of the kitchen.

She made arrangements for Tyler to stay overnight with Claire, Evan and Cody, then began the detailed procedure for dressing to go out for the evening. Because it was only four o'clock, she knew she would be ready early and might have to wait for Hunter who was still at the job site with Grant, but as far as she was concerned she needed the extra time. She needed the scented bath and the two hours of trying on clothes to calm herself and get herself acclimated to the fact that if she used caution and common sense and didn't push for too much too quickly from Hunter, all her dreams really could be coming true.

But when six o'clock turned into seven and seven turned into eight, Abby started to worry. She hadn't misinterpreted that he asked her out on a date. He said all the appropriate words—date, dinner, movie—and even set the time himself.

Convinced something was wrong, Abby had picked up the phone to call the construction trailer at the job site when Hunter strolled into the kitchen covered in mud.

"What the heck?" she said, replacing the receiver.

"We found a wetland," Hunter announced, obviously exasperated. "Can you believe—" He stopped suddenly and looked at her pale blue sweater and simple black skirt. Within seconds the confused look on his face turned to humiliation. He glanced down at his watch. "Damn," he whispered to himself. Then he looked up at her sheepishly. "Abby, I'm sorry."

Abby felt as if she had been swallowed whole by embarrassment, then she wished she would be swallowed whole by something...anything. He *forgot* that he had asked her out. How could a man *forget* he asked a woman for a date...unless he wasn't as excited about the date as she was...of course. He didn't want to go out with her. He'd only asked her out because he wanted her to marry him for Tyler's benefit. There hadn't been one ounce of romance in it.

She swallowed hard, then raised her chin. "Don't worry about it," she said nonchalantly, though Hunter could see from the expression on her face that she was upset. "It was a stupid idea anyway."

"No, it wasn't," he insisted, recognizing Tyler was going to be even more furious with him than Hunter was with himself. "It was a good idea because we need to get to know each other."

"We'll get to know each other very well by living together," Abby countered softly, opening the refrigerator. "You can use the downstairs bathroom to wash up. You probably have a clean set of clothes in the laundry room right beside it so you don't have to worry about changing. You can do it in the bathroom after you shower. I'll find something for you for dinner."

"Don't do that," Hunter said and almost closed her hand in the refrigerator when he slammed the door shut. "It's only eight o'clock. We still have plenty of time to run to the diner and get something to eat after I get dressed. It'll take me ten minutes, twenty tops."

When he saw his proposal wasn't having much impact, he lowered his voice and said, "Please. Please, Abby. I didn't do this on purpose. Things like this are very normal on a construction site. This job means a lot to both me and Grant, but it means a lot to the community, too. I couldn't just leave."

He deliberately neglected addressing that he'd forgotten their date and saw that by appealing to her sense of community he'd reached her. After all, the new mall he and Grant were building would mean plenty of jobs for Brewster County.

She sighed. "All right. You dress. I'll fix my make-up."

But the twenty minutes he needed to get dressed quickly turned into forty, and when he did arrive in the kitchen, Abby could see he was exhausted.

Adorable, but exhausted.

Wearing khaki pants and a green sweater that brought out all the best in his coloring, Hunter looked like a combination of a man of the world and a man very comfortable with who he was. Thinking that, Abby realized that by asking her out he more or less pushed himself into something that wasn't part of his nature. It did not come naturally for him to want to take her out. Which meant he wasn't attracted to her. The truth saddened her, but Abby had experienced enough disappointments in life that she knew better than to argue with it. She only accepted it. No matter how much it hurt.

Besides, it wasn't in *her* nature to allow someone to be miserable. Particularly not over her.

"I have fresh rolls from the bakery and a pound of ham if you'd like to have a sandwich here."

"No," he said, forcing a smile. "We can grab something at the diner."

"I'm sick of the diner," she said casually, giving him a good excuse to abandon the trip. "Besides," she said, smiling over at him, "I'm sort of tired. We can sit in the kitchen and talk just as easily as we can in a diner full of people. Probably more easily."

She saw that he debated, which was very sweet, but more than that it reminded her he was a good person. Because she genuinely believed he was an honest, honorable man, she wondered if he had it in him to be devious enough to ask her out only because he was trying to get her to marry him for Tyler's sake. She remembered the way he kissed her and she knew he had to have *some* feelings for her. A flicker of hope touched her heart. Maybe he really had forgotten?

"Okay. You're right. We can probably talk better here. Show me where everything is, and I'll make the sandwiches."

His offer to help was endearing. But he was tired. She could see the exhaustion in his eyes. She suspected volunteering to help had only been a courtesy, and she suddenly realized that was their real problem. They were so concerned with perceptions, neither one of them acted honestly. If they were ever going to get to know each other, they had to start being honest and stop doing what each thought was expected. The best way to do that would be to forget the past, put the future on hold and deal in the present. Surely they could handle that.

"Why don't you sit and let me make the sandwiches?"

Obviously grateful for the opportunity to rest, he peered at her. "You're sure?"

"Of course, I'm sure," she said with a laugh, glad Hunter had been honest on his own without her having to make an explanation. She walked to the refrigerator to retrieve the sandwich supplies. "I don't remember your being this helpful before."

"I probably wasn't. But after enough years of being in business for myself, I quickly learned to just jump in and do what needs to be done."

"No kidding," Abby agreed as she began to arrange the ham and bread. "I think that's why they like me so much at the diner. I don't wait to be told about anything. Having been in charge of the bed-and-breakfast for so long, I also know to jump in and do something when there's a problem or work that needs to be done.''

Abby asked his preference of condiments and Hunter told her he liked mustard and cheese. As she handed him a plate with two sandwiches she asked, "So why was finding a wetland significant?"

"Wetlands are endangered in this country and protected by federal laws. We've decided to build away from it rather than disturb it.''

"Sounds like a good decision.''

"I'm sure it is, since it was Grant's call. He typically handles the actual on-site work. I've been out of it for years.'' He paused and smiled at Abby. "But it felt so good to be outside again, to wear coveralls and boots and talk to men about dirt that I wonder if I'll ever be able to face another accountant or lawyer again.''

Abby loved the bright tone of his voice. She loved the sparkle in his eyes. If she hadn't already gotten over her anger, those gray-green eyes would have made it impossible for her to stay mad at him, but more than that they made her curious. "So you do the business with the accountants and lawyers?''

"Yeah, hard to believe, isn't it?'' he said, in between bites of sandwich. She could see he'd worked up a ravenous appetite from the day's work and automatically rose to make him more sandwiches.

"I was undoubtedly voted most likely to fail and Grant was virtually born with enough savvy to be an accountant or lawyer, but I'm the one who ends up negotiating contracts and examining budgets with them.''

Abby laughed. "You were never voted most likely

to fail. As I recall, you had enough ambition for three people.''

He didn't say anything for so long that Abby realized he was waiting for her to look at him. When she glanced up and caught his gaze, he said, "If I had confidence and ambition, it was thanks to you."

With her decision to deal only in present-day reality firmly in place, Abby did not want to take another trip back to the past and get confused again. She brushed his praise aside. "Not really. You always knew who you wanted to be."

"Yeah, but I wasn't really sure I could make it until I started hanging out with you and you continually pointed out my good traits."

"Well, it's just nice to see everything worked out for you," Abby said, busying herself with his sandwiches. She wasn't surprised that he immediately began to eat them the minute she set the second plate in front of him.

"I only wish things could have worked out as well for you."

"Oh, don't worry about me," Abby said, cheerfully dismissing his concern as she had done with his praise because that was another side road she didn't care to venture down. Her life while he was away consisted of her parents' illnesses and her daydreams that he would someday return for her. Neither topic was appropriate at this point. "Tell me more about your day."

"Like what?"

"Like what a grown man could be doing that would get him covered with mud."

"Identifying flora and fauna."

That made her giggle. "Identifying what?"

"Well, before we decided to work around the wetland, we had a specialist walking through that area with us identifying the plant life and even some of the insects and animals." He paused and shook his head. "When these guys say they get down and dirty with their work, they aren't kidding. He had me looking under leaves, lying on the ground so I didn't disturb any possible insects underneath...."

Abby laughed again. "No way."

"It's true," he said, then stopped and stretched as if incredibly uncomfortable. "I think that's why my back is so stiff right now."

"Here, let me," Abby said, pushing his hands away and replacing them with her own. She tried not to notice how wonderful his supple flesh felt beneath her fingers, tried not to make too much out of his groan of pleasure.

"That feels wonderful."

"You must be very tired."

"I am."

He said it in such a way that Abby felt as if he'd shared a confidence with her and realized he was careful not to let anyone see a sign of weakness. Admitting he was tired was something like a compliment.

Maybe there was hope for them after all?

"I'm not accustomed to working in the field, but I think I may have to get used to it. This project's bigger than anything Grant and I have tackled before. For every bit as exciting as that is, it also makes me a little nervous."

Another concession. Another compliment of sorts. Abby smiled. "Millions of dollars are at stake. I should think you would be a little nervous."

"The money's an issue," Hunter admitted, as Abby

continued to work his muscles. He leaned a little closer to give her better access and Abby let her hands glide toward the small of his back, reveling in the intimacy that was developing between them.

"But it's not as much of an issue as disappointing the community. If this mall doesn't take off, people will lose their newfound jobs, businessmen and women who put in shops will lose their investments and the community will lose tax revenue."

"And it won't be the end of the world," Abby soothed. "Not only will everybody survive, but, personally, I don't think you're going to fail."

He stopped her ministrations by grabbing her hand, and turned on his chair to face her. "You really don't, do you?"

"Heavens, no," she said, laughing slightly at his very serious expression, though the touch of his hand holding hers sent shivers up her arm and the intimacy of the conversation warmed her all over. "You had the tenacity and perseverance of three people when you left here seven years ago. Lots of things about you might have changed, but I don't think anybody can take away good character traits."

For several seconds he only studied her, then he smiled ruefully. "Thank you."

She stared at him. "For believing in you?"

He nodded.

"That's always come very naturally to me."

Hunter smiled. Abby smiled. For the first time since he returned she wasn't nervous or anxious, only happy. And he wasn't pushy or analytical, only real. She was talking to the real Hunter Wyman tonight. And it felt so darned good.

Hunter cleared his throat as if to break the silence

that had developed between them, then said, "Like I said before, I wish things could've turned out as well for you and Tyler as they did for me."

Abby had precluded him from taking them down this road before, and she hadn't changed her mind about discussing the more painful parts of her past. She also wasn't about to let him wallow in misery for something that wasn't his fault. "Tyler and I have more than survived—we've been happy and that's what counts."

"There's more to being happy than you think, Abby."

Confused by his tone, Abby glanced at him. "What do you mean by that?"

"Well, it seems to me that Tyler is very concerned about you."

At that Abby smiled. "I know."

"No, I mean *really* concerned about you," Hunter said. "More concerned than a six-year-old should be."

Recognition of why he had made that statement sent a tingle of suspicion through Abby. "You've been talking about me?"

"He only wanted to make sure I knew my place."

"So that's why the two of you bonded so quickly," she realized aloud, amazed she hadn't seen this sooner.

"He wanted to make sure that I appreciated you and did right by you."

For Abby, the tingle of suspicion became full-scale understanding. "And did doing right by me involve asking me out?"

"He just wanted assurance that I wouldn't try to get something for nothing," Hunter said with a groan. "Come on, Abby, this is guy stuff. He was protecting

one of his own. To Tyler, I'm an intruder. He only
wanted me to follow the rules.''

"I see,'' Abby said stiffly.

"No, you don't. You're taking this all wrong.
You're taking it like...a woman,'' he said, exasperated.

"That might be because I am a woman,'' Abby replied, walking away from his chair, since she was getting the sudden urge to take her fingers off his back
and wrap them around his neck. She could understand
Tyler not realizing that coaxing Hunter into asking her
out would be humiliating, but Hunter was old enough
to understand. "I'm so mad and so embarrassed,'' she
said, tossing her hands in the air, "that I don't know
which one of you to strangle.''

"You shouldn't strangle either of us. Both of our
intentions were good. Even when we went to the Petersons to order flowers, Tyler was prompting me because he wanted you to be taken care of.''

At that, Abby's mouth fell open in indignation. "*He*
prompted you to send me to the flowers?''

Hunter had the good graces to look sheepish. "I
would have thought of it myself eventually, Abby. But
you're missing the point. My listening to Tyler and
working with Tyler about his needs—which just happen to involve you primarily—is my way of edging
myself into his world. There was nothing sinister about
it.''

"And nothing romantic, either,'' Abby said, her
voice wobbling. She didn't know whether to die of
embarrassment or sadness. Every time she thought
there was hope for her and Hunter it turned out that
he wasn't the man she thought he was. A six-year-old
boy had to tell him to send her flowers. It was so

humiliating, she could have happily gone to her room and stayed there forever.

"Come on, Abby," Hunter cajoled, rising and walking toward her. "You know I meant every ounce of sentiment behind those flowers."

"Oh, yeah?" Abby said, tilting her head up to look at him. "Red roses symbolize passion and from where I stand I don't see one passionate bone in your body."

"Why? Because I took the advice of a friend?" He paused and ran his hand across the back of his neck. "I'm not sure what you want from me. What in the hell else am I supposed to do to make you see I'm interested? I sent you flowers. I asked you out. True, I came home too late to make good on the promise of a movie, but despite the fact that I was tired I was ready, willing and able to take you somewhere."

"Oh, that makes me feel peachy," Abby said, just barely keeping her voice below a shout. "Why don't you come right out and say I'm a charity case?"

"What?" Hunter gasped and this time Abby saw his eyes were beginning to blaze with fury.

"Face it, Hunter," Abby said. "I'm your son's mother, a woman you haven't seen in seven years and someone you would like to marry for convenience. You might not see me as a charity case, but I'd bet my bottom dollar you don't see me as very much beyond that."

Before Abby knew what hit her, Hunter grabbed her shoulders and yanked her up for a long, openmouthed kiss. Because the kiss was so sudden, Abby didn't have time to think about how she should react. All she could do was react. And react she did. Not only did she kiss him back every bit as fiercely and furiously as he was kissing her, but by the time he pulled away, every bone and muscle in her body had turned to gelatin. Heat suffused her and rational thought did not have a hope of life in her brain.

"Is that the way a man kisses a woman he considers a charity case?" Hunter asked, taking her chin and tipping it upward so he could see her eyes.

She swallowed.

"That's exactly what I thought," he said, then released her and walked out of the kitchen. She heard his bedroom door slam, then nothing but the tick of the old kitchen clock.

She stood speechless, confused and just about certain she was losing her marbles. With her dreams of fairy-tale romance long gone and a marriage of convenience out of the question unless they learned to communicate better, she didn't know what was left for them anymore.

But she did know one thing: if there was half as much passion and emotion in the things he said and did as there was in his kisses, he could promise her the moon and she would believe him.

And that might actually be worse.

Chapter Five

When Hunter arrived in the kitchen the next morning, Abby turned from the eggs she was frying. "Good morning," she said cheerfully, hoping that by ignoring what had happened the night before it would simply go away.

No such luck. Pulling out a chair, Hunter didn't even look at her when he gruffly said, "Good morning."

"Hey, Hunter," Tyler said. Kneeling on the seat directly across the table from his father, his eyes bright, his smile wide, Abby and Hunter's little boy appeared to be the happiest child on the face of the earth.

"Hey, Tyler," Hunter said, as Abby set a plate of bacon and eggs in front of him. "How was your evening with Claire and Evan?"

"Fun," Tyler replied simply. "They have Cody at night, you know," he said, referring to the fact that Evan and Claire took charge of one of Evan's deceased father's triplets. "He's funny. He falls on his butt when he tries to walk, then he cries."

"He's a baby," Abby said with a laugh, ruffling Tyler's hair. "I hope you didn't make fun of him."

"No, I just picked him up and helped him stand again."

"That's nice," Abby said as she joined her son and Hunter.

After the short discussion of Tyler's time away, the breakfast table grew quiet. Abby searched her brain for something to say, but she couldn't stop thinking about that kiss from the night before. Worse, Hunter's sullen attitude only compounded her confusion. All the cards always appeared to be stacked against Hunter until he kissed her. He didn't kiss her like a man only interested in her in order to give Tyler a family. Passionate kisses like that resulted from chemistry. And though chemistry wasn't love, it was certainly a sign of attraction.

"Run upstairs and get your things," Hunter said to Tyler, sounding so much like a father who had been with his son from the beginning that Abby was momentarily taken aback. "Then I'll walk you to school."

"That's not necessary," Abby protested, but Hunter shot her a warning look.

"I know it's not necessary," he said, as Tyler scampered out of the room. "It's something I *want* to do."

She knew he was making a correlation between his treatment of Tyler and his feelings for her and Abby quickly looked away. If she judged only by his anger this morning and the way he kissed her, she would believe he desired her for herself, not merely because she was the mother of his child. But she couldn't go by two pieces of evidence. Too many other things had happened. Not the least of which was that Hunter had needed the advice of her son to woo her. She could consider that he had been so busy over the past few years, he didn't remember how to be good to a woman anymore and forgive him. Or she could conclude that though they had sexual chemistry, she didn't inspire him to great heights of emotion, and realize that probably meant he didn't have feelings for her.

She didn't know which it was. The only thing that was clear to her was that the old Hunter, the Hunter who had loved her seven years ago, never had a problem showering her with affection. And since nothing but kisses came naturally to the new Hunter, she had to assume he had changed so much that he was no longer the man she had once loved. If she married him for Tyler's sake, she would be marrying a stranger.

She almost discussed the situation with the Brewster women when they brought the triplets in for breakfast that morning, but decided against it. She was confused enough without getting three more opinions. But as she talked with them while they fed their children, Abby was struck with an intense desire to have a baby again. The feeling was so strong, she suddenly began to see that getting involved with Hunter, specifically marrying Hunter, had some ramifications and repercussions she had never considered.

For one, he would want a real marriage. This would be no marriage of convenience. That would mean more children. Even as the idea of more babies overwhelmed her with happiness, she also recognized that additional children would have a huge impact on Tyler. Though having his parents marry should be a good thing, having siblings when he was well accustomed to being a pampered only child might not be an easy thing for him to bear. What if they married and had more children and Tyler rebelled?

Or what if this new Hunter had some radical ideas about raising children that he hadn't yet shared with her?

Worse, what if he had changed his ideas about life in general? Given how differently he behaved, he could hold entirely opposite beliefs from the ones they had shared seven years ago.

How could she have more kids with a man she didn't know?

Swamped by all the potential problems that accompanied marrying a virtual stranger, Abby decided right then and there that they had to forget—*forget*—about getting married. If they put that one issue behind them, not only would it remove negative complications for Tyler, but she would have less chance of getting her heart broken.

And she had to concede that was the real, bottom-line issue. If she chose to marry this man, she would put her whole heart and soul into the marriage and she wasn't sure Hunter was capable of returning the favor. Oh, he would take care of her. He would make sure she never did without. And they would probably have a stunning sex life. But without the love, without the tenderness they had known, without the sweetness and generosity, it would be hollow. And Abby didn't want hollow. If the purpose of Hunter's return to her life was to show her how much he had changed and to prove that he wasn't her Prince Charming, then she had to realize it was time to get on with the rest of her life…with someone else.

The truth was, Hunter's return could actually be the end of their relationship, not a new beginning.

But when he arrived home that evening, in time for supper, and carrying a bouquet of wildflowers, all her wonderful reasoning flew out of her head.

This was something the old Hunter would have done.

"What are these?" she asked slowly, then swallowed hard as he handed them to her.

"They're wildflowers from the wetland. I thought you would like them."

The simplicity of it touched her and reminded her so much of the kinds of things he had done when they were younger, that she blinked rapidly to prevent tears from forming in her eyes. She didn't know what had happened to him in the intervening years, but these flowers almost made up for it.

"I do like them. They're beautiful."

"And I've also made dinner reservations for us."

Her gaze jerked from the flowers to his face.

"And I've hired a baby-sitter. Someone recommended by Grant's housekeeper, Mrs. Romani."

She almost succumbed to the sweetness of that. All those things were so much like the old Hunter that she could have fallen into his arms with relief. But the new Hunter was a shrewd businessman. He would recognize his mistakes from the night before and simply correct them. As sweet and adorable as all this appeared, it might be nothing more than a correction of problems by a man very determined to get what he wanted.

She swallowed. "All this is very nice, Hunter," she said, her voice a hoarse whisper. "But I did a little thinking today and I saw that everything between us is only strained because we keep trying to revive a dead romance.''

He began to protest, but Abby stopped him with a wave of her hand. ''You and Tyler get along well. You and I get along well when we're talking about Tyler. You and Tyler and I get along well as a family.'' She swallowed again. ''It's only when you and I try to make us something more that we run into difficulties.

''So, for Tyler's sake, I think we should forget about getting married.''

Hunter cursed, then shook his head and caught her gaze. ''You know what? I don't buy that.''

His anger changed her sadness into confusion and she gaped at him. ''Don't buy what? I'm not asking you to change an opinion. I stated a fact. We all get along very, very well until you and I talk marriage, then everything goes haywire.''

''Oh, I agree with all that. But I don't agree that you're doing this for Tyler.''

Shocked, she pressed her hand to her chest. ''It's true.''

He shook his head dejectedly. ''No, it isn't. The truth is that you don't want to get hurt, so you won't even try. You won't even give me a chance to win you over to my way of thinking.''

If he had said to win her *love*, Abby realized, she might have given in. But when he said to win her over to his way of thinking, Abby was unexpectedly heart-broken. She hadn't realized how very much she wanted him to say that one little four-letter word. And she also recognized that that was the problem. Seven years ago, she had no doubt that he loved her—until he left town. When he left, admittedly with sufficient reason, she suddenly felt he didn't love her. Now, he was back, ready to marry her, and she didn't know what to do.

She desperately needed for him to convince her that he *loved* her, that he had loved her when he left and that he would always love her. But the best he could do was try to win her to his way of thinking.

Proud, hurt, she looked up into his beautiful eyes. "I don't want to be won over to your way of thinking," she said, holding his gaze. "If and when I marry, it will be for love, because no matter what you think, it wouldn't be good for Tyler to see a loveless marriage. So I won't marry you. Not this week, not next. Because whether you understand it or not, I refuse to do anything that will hurt Tyler. If you still want to stay in the bed-and-breakfast, I think that's a good idea. But there will be no personal relationship between us. And that's the deal. You can take it or leave it."

"You know what, Abby?" Hunter said as he picked up his jacket from the chair on which he had dropped it. "I think I'll leave it. I'll find somewhere else to stay and you and I can work out visitation arrangements for Tyler because I think your deal stinks."

Then he surprised her by grabbing her hand and putting the flowers in it. "I picked these for you," he said, "because they reminded me of you and because I knew you would love them. They're yours."

With that he turned and walked out the door, fully determined never to look back. Oh, he knew he would have to return to get his things, but that was it. If Abby hadn't confirmed the opinion he'd acquired of relationships during his first marriage, nothing would ever confirm it. Not because she rejected his affections, though she had and that hurt, but because she was obstinate. If she couldn't have things her way, she didn't want them any way at all.

With nowhere to go, Hunter drove to Brewster mansion. Grant opened the door after Hunter rang the bell.

"What's up?" he asked, inviting Hunter into the foyer.

"I'm bored. I need some work to do."

"Well, I can certainly help you with that," Grant said, laughing as Hunter shrugged out of his jacket. "Let's go to the den."

Hunter followed Grant down the long corridor to the large den. When Grant strode around the mahogany desk and took the burgundy leather seat behind it, Hunter automatically sat in the chair in front of it.

Riffling through some papers, Grant said, "So, you and Abby have a fight?"

Not really in the mood to discuss it, Hunter squeezed the armrest. "No."

"Oh," Grant said, still wading through papers and blueprints. "That's odd because that would be the only reason I could see for you giving up an opportunity to spend time with Tyler."

"Tyler's not home. He's out playing with friends."

Grant glanced up. "This late at night?"

"It's not—" Hunter peered out the window and saw the darkness. "I guess it is."

"So, where's Tyler, then?"

Hunter squirmed on his seat. "I don't know. Abby and I had our fight before I could ask."

"Relax," Grant said, obviously seeing his friend's discomfort. "It's not easy getting used to being a father. You should have seen me, Evan and Chas the first week we had the triplets. Couldn't boil water and we were in charge of three babies. It was a hoot. Thank God we had Claire.''

"How'd you get adjusted?"

"Trial and error...and repetition. You do anything enough times and eventually it'll come automatically.''

"That doesn't excuse me, Grant. I should be smart enough to ask about my son before I go barreling out of the house.''

"Three times everybody made plans without ever once considering the triplets. If we hadn't caught the mistake, we would have left three babies home alone.'' Grant paused in his paper search and sighed. "Forgive yourself and move on.''

"That's just it. I'm not sure how to move on. I think I burned one too many bridges tonight when I told Abby I was finding somewhere else to stay and that we could work out some kind of visitation agreement.''

"Ouch!'' Kristen, Grant's wife, said from the den door. "Hunter, that's just plain mean.''

"I didn't intend to be mean,'' Hunter said. "It just all came out before I could stop it.''

"Give me some specifics and let me see if I can figure out what happened,'' Kristen suggested kindly.

Hunter shook his head. "I'd rather not. At this point, I'd like to keep things between Abby and me. And I'd like something to do,'' he reminded Grant, nodding at the stack of papers on his desk.

"What you need to do is go back and work things out with Abby,'' Grant began.

Hunter interrupted him. "I need to work, Grant. I just need to work. Work is the only thing that's ever really made sense to me. It's the only thing I can control. It got me respect. It gave me self-esteem. I want to work."

"Do you want to work, or do you want to hide in work?"

"Grant, just give me the specifications for the structural steel so I can start writing the request for bids."

Grant stared at his friend, but Hunter didn't flinch. Finally, Grant gave up and found the documents. Hunter bundled them up and started up the hall to the front door. When he arrived, Kristen was waiting for him, holding his jacket.

"You know, sugar," she said, her Texas accent honey sweet, "you can stay here if you like. We have plenty of room."

Hunter drew a long breath. "Tempting as that is, I don't think so. I had a hotel before I went to the bed-and-breakfast. I'll be fine there again."

Chapter Six

Hunter hadn't slept at the bed-and-breakfast the night before, but because Abby knew he would return for his belongings, she was expecting him when he showed up in her kitchen after work. Covered in mud and looking exhausted, he pushed open her back door.

"Hi."

"Hi," she said, wiping her hands on her apron.

"I just came to get my things," he said carefully, motioning toward the hallway. Then, as if realizing that he would be tromping his mud-covered body through her house, he glanced down at himself and grimaced. "Maybe this isn't such a good idea right now?"

Actually, Abby figured there was no time like the present. Not only was Tyler outside with his friends, but if she remembered their argument correctly, he had decided to leave because she refused to let him live in her home if he didn't abide by a purely platonic relationship with her. Since he insisted on going, she was afraid that meant he intended to pursue her. And she wasn't having any part of that. As far as she was concerned, he had already proven he was no longer the man she loved. If she took up with him now, she would be taking up with a stranger.

Best to get him out of the house before the situation got any more confused than it already was.

"How about this?" Abby suggested. "You take a shower in the bathroom off the laundry room and I'll go upstairs and get something for you to change into."

He smiled sheepishly. "That would work. Then I could clear out my room. I'll call you about seeing Tyler."

His politeness gave her a pang of regret for her own lack of hospitality, particularly since his being in her home was more about Tyler and Hunter getting to know each other than her relationship with Hunter. "Or you could stay for supper first. Tyler would like that. You could even help him with homework, and we could discuss visitation before you leave."

"Okay," he said, nodding.

"Okay," Abby agreed awkwardly. "I'll set your clothes outside the bathroom door. Supper will be ready in about twenty minutes."

Hunter turned toward the laundry room and Abby left the kitchen to go upstairs to retrieve his clothes. She entered his room without any qualm of conscience. But when she found all the dresser drawers empty and realized she would have to poke through his suitcases, she was stabbed by uneasiness that she was invading his privacy, intruding into his life when he didn't want her there. At least not in the personal, intimate way she had been seven years ago. And she recognized that was really what troubled her. He held himself so tightly in reserve that she knew she would never get close to him again, and it hurt that he didn't want to be close to her.

But as she rummaged to find a shirt and trousers, Abby was struck by another, clearer thought. What if their inability to get along wasn't because Hunter didn't want her intruding into his life as much as he didn't have much of a life for her to intrude into? The only things about which he spoke with passion were his business and their son. The fact that Hunter lived out of a suitcase might be an indication that he was a lot more alone, and maybe even lonelier, than anybody knew.

She dismissed that thought, relegating it into the none-of-her-business corner of her brain, gathered his clothes and set them outside the bathroom door as she promised, then went back to her cooking. Tyler bounded into the kitchen, and Abby ordered him upstairs to clean up for dinner. As she was about to put the finishing touches on the food, both Tyler and Hunter stood before her, clean and ready to eat.

"I'll get the plates," Hunter said automatically.

"I'll get the silverware," Tyler volunteered happily.

"Okay, I'll put dinner on the table, then," Abby said. Her comfort level actually increased with the belief that Hunter wasn't so much private and emotionless as he was alone or without deep, dark secrets and passions to share. The proprietor of a bed-and-breakfast, she knew all about putting people at ease, and, as long as she thought of Hunter as a tired lonely guest, she knew exactly how to get along with him.

After they sat down to eat, she said, "So, how was your day?"

Hunter said, "Busy," at the same time that Tyler said, "Lousy."

Both Hunter and Abby turned their attention to Tyler. "What do you mean lousy?" Hunter asked before Abby had a chance to say anything.

"Jimmy Parker called me dumb."

"You're not dumb," Abby said, then speared a potato with her fork. "Just ignore him."

"He said I was a big, *fat* dummy."

"You're also not fat," Abby said. "And you know Jimmy Parker can be a bully sometimes. Just ignore him and he'll be back to normal in a few days."

But as Abby gave her sensible instructions, Hunter's eyes narrowed. "How long has this boy been picking on you?"

"Forever," Tyler said.

"How long is forever?" Hunter asked simply.

"Since pre-kindergarten," Abby replied absently, believing Hunter was only seeking information, not realizing he was out for blood.

Unfortunately, his next comment clearly signaled trouble. "Parker?" Hunter said. His face drawn into a thoughtful expression, Hunter couldn't hide the fact that he was plotting revenge. "Is he the son of the Parkers who run the bank?"

"Grandson," Abby supplied. "But there's no need to go overboard," she said carefully. "Remember these are six-year-old boys you're talking about. In a few days this will blow over."

But with Hunter's defensive reaction to Tyler's problem, all the puzzle pieces had finally fallen into place in Abby's head. For the first time since Hunter returned home she felt that she not only had a handle on what was going on, but also that she had some control. Hunter was a single man who ran a company that took so much of his time he didn't have a personal life. With Tyler, Hunter had a personal life. Things to look forward to. Someone to love. That was why Tyler was so important to him. Hunter was even willing to marry a woman he didn't know to keep the boy in his life and to get daily doses of love from him.

"This time tomorrow Jimmy Parker could be one of Tyler's best friends. They fight all the time because they're the smartest two kids in their class. Sometimes it makes them friends, but sometimes it brings out a competitive streak."

"Competitive streak?" Hunter asked, happily curious.

"Yes, Hunter, Tyler has a competitive streak," Abby said, laughing. "He's all boy."

"Do you play any sports yet?" Hunter asked him. Tyler grinned. "T-ball."

"The season starts right after school lets out," Abby explained, seeing Hunter light up at this news and knowing her suspicions were correct. Hunter *needed* to be a part of Tyler's life.

When dinner was finished, Abby suggested that she clean the kitchen while Hunter help Tyler with his homework. Again, Hunter eagerly agreed. As she washed their dishes and wiped down the stove and counter tops, Abby watched her son blossom under Hunter's approval. She watched as he enjoyed the company of another male. She watched him giggle and struggle and just plain be happy, even as Hunter virtually glowed.

And she knew what she had to do.

When she sent Tyler to his room to begin prepara-

tions for his bath, and Hunter announced he would go
upstairs to get his things, Abby stopped him.

"Don't," she said, shaking her head.

He frowned. "Don't what?"

"Don't leave," she said, drawing a resigned breath.
"Tyler adores you. You adore Tyler. You need some
time to bond. The best way for you to get that time
would be for you to continue living here."

"Are you sure?" Hunter asked quietly.

She nodded, then glanced up at him and smiled. But
when she actually looked into his eyes and saw the
serious, concerned expression, Abby had her first set
of second thoughts, even as she felt a wave of attraction that had nothing to do with the past. He wasn't
the man he had been seven years ago, the man she
loved. But he was still a good, honest, decent man.
Maturity had added a dimension to his integrity that
he didn't have when he left and in some ways that
made him even more attractive than he had been.

Add that to his good looks, sex appeal and the
charm she knew still lurked in the depths of his per-
sonality and Abby realized something that she hadn't
considered before this. Even if he had changed, she
could easily love the new man he had become. Maybe
more than she had loved the boy who had left her.

But she wasn't sure this man could love her. She
wasn't sure he could love anybody but Tyler. She'd
seen the sparse way he lived. His only real conversations had been about work. She didn't know what he
had done in the past seven years, except that he had
become overwhelmingly successful. And though a
woman would have to wonder how she could love
somebody who didn't seem to see any farther than the
spreadsheets and contracts in front of his nose, Abby

suddenly saw that was part of what attracted her to him. He needed her. And being needed by him was every bit as alluring as the intense desire to marry him in the hope of reviving their love. Having him continue to live in her house would only magnify those temptations.

Of course, she was a mature adult, who was supposed to be able to sort through things like this and keep her wits about her, and a mother who had to put the welfare of her child before her own personal concerns.

She nodded again. "I'm sure," she said, then paused and caught his gaze again. "But, Hunter, I haven't changed my mind from last night. If anything, I think we need to have a few ground rules."

"Ground rules?"

"Not just for you and Tyler, but for you and me."

"I understand your wanting ground rules for Tyler and me. I don't want to undermine anything you've taught him." He paused, and blew his breath out on a sigh because he completely lost his train of thought. What he wanted to do right now was kiss her. Her mouth was about six inches below his because, as always when she wanted to make a point, Abby was up close and personal. He couldn't stop thinking about the kisses they'd shared, about the fact that she still felt something for him, about the fact that she could make him go up in flames with a look from her innocent eyes. But, unfortunately, it was the last thought that always brought him back to earth.

She had wonderfully innocent eyes because she was an innocent person. She still believed in love and goodness and the kind of romances that happened in fairy tales, and he had finally figured out that was what she wanted from him. But he didn't believe in love. The only goodness he had ever found in this world he had found with her. And as far as he was concerned, romance died. It always did. Even their passionate romance had ended. They were no longer the match made in heaven they had once been, and if he married her, even for Tyler's sake, he might hurt her. He didn't want to hurt her. Never, not even accidentally.

Taking a pace back, he swallowed hard and said, "I also understand needing ground rules for you and me." He not only knew they couldn't turn back the clock to what they'd had seven years ago, he also knew it was more his fault than hers. He couldn't change his opinion about life, about love, about people. The damage had been done.

"And you're willing to go along with what I want?"

"Yes," he said, mostly because he refused to hurt her. If they married, she would go into the marriage wholeheartedly, idealistically, and when she discovered he couldn't reciprocate her unconditional love, she would be hurt.

But as quickly as he reminded himself of that, he also realized that wasn't necessarily true. At least it was not unequivocally true that the only thing she would get out of the marriage was pain. She was as alone as he was now. She was single, broke and struggling to raise a child. Given enough time, she would undoubtedly see that if she married him, he would make her life easy. He could give her everything she wanted, solve her financial problems, make it possible for her to quit working at the diner, and take half the burden of raising Tyler. With as genuinely difficult as her life was, Hunter couldn't believe that a marriage would only be bad for her. And eventually even she would have to see the benefits.

He almost groaned at his stupidity. He had been going about this all wrong. He had pushed her too far, too fast, without giving her enough time to draw the natural, logical conclusions so obvious to him.

Their last kiss popped up in his memory and he didn't remember the passion, he felt it. Every blistering tingle assaulted him. But more than that, the fact that she answered his kiss haunted him. She definitely felt something for him. It couldn't be love after only a little over a week in each other's company, but she felt enough that with time he could easily show her that a marriage between them would work.

Without any effort on his part, a plan formed for how he could convince her that respect, friendship and creature comforts were better things to base a marriage on than love. But he knew he had to agree to keep their relationship platonic to remain close to her so he could implement his plan. In fact, the best way to implement it would be by keeping their relationship platonic so she would clearly see the other things he was offering her.

"Okay, you're right. I do want to know Tyler. I can see Tyler wants to know me. Your rules," he said, then turned and walked out of the room because he suddenly felt like a little boy who had lied to his favorite teacher.

Technically, he wasn't deceiving her. He was simply giving her time to get to know him again so that she could see he was a safe bet as marriage material. He might not be able to give her a fairy-tale romance, but he could take care of her and Tyler.

Since she was a grown-up now, no longer eighteen,

she would soon realize that in the real world that was
what counted.

"Mom! Mom! Get up! Hunter's making pancakes!"

Abby groggily opened her eyes and turned her head
to look at her alarm clock. When she saw it was almost
eight thirty, she jumped out of bed and ran to her door.
"Tyler!" she gasped. "Oh, my gosh! Go back to your
bedroom and throw on some clothes! You're going to
be late for school."

Tyler giggled merrily. "No, I'm not! It's Saturday."

Combing her fingers through her tangled hair, Abby
stopped dead in her tracks and said, "So it is."

"And Hunter's making pancakes."

"Oh, yeah?" Abby said, frozen to the spot in the
upstairs hall, trying to orient herself.

"Yeah," Tyler said. "And he said if you want to
get one hot off the grill you have to come down in the
next five minutes."

Abby cleared her throat. "Okay, tell him I'll be
right down."

But in the shower Abby experienced a moment of
sheer panic. The past three weeks had been wonderful.
For the first time in his life, Tyler had a father and he
reveled in it. Hunter was happy. Tyler was happy. And
she, well, she was getting panicky.

The truth was that they were making a family. The
only step they hadn't taken was for her and Hunter to
become romantically involved. But she was tempted.
And that was the problem. Or at least part of the problem. The other part was Tyler.

The bed-and-breakfast hadn't had a guest since
Hunter moved in, but she hadn't had to scrimp and

save because Hunter was making up the difference. He walked Tyler to school. He bought Tyler a new jacket, shoes and jeans. His laundry was mingled in with hers and Tyler's. After three weeks of near familial bliss, Abby couldn't help but wonder what Tyler was making of all this.

In the kitchen, seeing Hunter by the stove, spatula in hand, pancakes sizzling on the griddle and a giggling child by his side, Abby wondered if she wasn't worried for nothing. Hunter was happy. Tyler was thrilled. She was getting pancakes. Why upset the applecart?

"Where did you learn to make pancakes?" she asked to announce herself, and both Hunter and Tyler turned from the stove to grin at her.

"Living alone," Hunter supplied easily. "I'm an excellent cook."

"So I see," Abby said, remembering the wonderful things he had done with dinner the few nights he had come home early enough to help her. "I'll get the dishes," she said, but noticed they were already on the table. "Oh."

"I get everything ready beforehand."

"Organized," Abby said, and took a seat at the table. With Hunter behaving like the perfect gentleman and looking like every woman's fantasy come to life— with his perfect gray-green eyes, perfect body and perfect contented smile as he made perfect pancakes—it was hard to focus solely on Tyler and even harder to remind herself that this was simply supposed to be a platonic relationship. Particularly since Hunter hadn't wanted a platonic relationship. She was the one who set that rule. And after three happy weeks with him, she couldn't remember why.

Watching him, she allowed herself the luxury of wondering what it might have been like if she had agreed to marry him when he had asked and instantly heat suffused her. Even though he didn't love her, he was sweet, sexy and so handsome he took her breath away. Surely over the course of time, he could grow to love her. He had loved her once…and he had kissed her like a man who could find his passion for life again, given half a chance—

She stopped herself. If she married him exactly as he was now, he would have no reason to find his passion because he would have everything he wanted. Tyler. Her. Marriage. Home. Security. He would have no need for the intense, intimate love that she wanted so badly from him and she would be in exactly the same position she was in right now.

Except she would be getting those wonderful kisses…and making love, she realized. The mere thought caused her to shiver.

Luckily, Hunter didn't notice. "Being organized isn't a crime."

"Yeah, it isn't a crime," Tyler parroted and Abby laughed, grateful to come out of her thoughts.

Within minutes, Hunter had breakfast served. Abby sipped hot spicy coffee, ate moist delicious pancakes and thought she'd died and gone to heaven. If she agreed to marry him, she could have breakfasts like this every Saturday, but she would never have his love.

"Tyler, if you're not doing anything special, I thought you might like to go to the construction site with me this morning," Hunter said, and Abby almost choked on her coffee.

"He can't go to a construction site!"

Hunter said, "Sure he can," at the same time that Tyler said, "Aw, Mom!"

"I mean it, Tyler! You're too young. You could get hurt."

"Not on a Saturday," Hunter assured. "None of the equipment will be running. None of the workers will be on-site. It'll only be Grant and me, working on a few requests for bids. And I won't be there long. Only until noon. Not enough time for Tyler to get bored."

He said the last with a lightly coaxing voice and Abby simply stared at him. She wanted to give him every possible minute with his son, and she knew that Hunter would be careful with Tyler's safety, but the second she looked into his beautiful gray-green eyes, she lost all coherent thought. She remembered kissing him those first few days after he had arrived home, and all the feelings came flooding back as if she were kissing him now, instead of remembering.

"Please, Mom?"

Tyler's voice interrupted Abby's thoughts and she shook her head to bring herself back into reality.

"All right. You guys go on. I'll clean the kitchen."

"And then we'll take you to lunch," Hunter said, as if he had only decided it on the spot.

Abby gave him a look that warned him not to overstep his boundaries, and with the look he returned he told her that he knew the rules. She sighed. "All right," she agreed.

But when Hunter directed Tyler to the door and the pair walked out of the kitchen into the bright May sunshine, Abby experienced a quick flash of bad feelings. She wondered again what kind of impression she and Hunter were giving Tyler, then decided that he was too young to even think about most of her concerns.

"I've had a change of heart about our relationship."

Hunter looked up from the report he was reading on the back porch swing. Abby stood before him, dressed in jeans and a simple T-shirt, her voluminous hair flowing around her. His breath caught in his throat and he swallowed hard. The moment he had worked for for three long weeks was finally at hand. He could feel it in his bones.

"Sit," he said, patting the swing beside him, keeping the eagerness out of his voice only with great effort.

Obviously nervous, she perched herself on the swing. Before she spoke, she ran her tongue across her lips. "I'm concerned about the impression we're giving Tyler."

Hunter couldn't help it, he laughed. "What could possibly be wrong with the impression we're giving Tyler? If anything, he should think he's the luckiest kid on the face of the earth."

She licked her lips again. "That's just it. With us not having an honest relationship, we're setting up a false impression about what life is like between a man and woman who live together."

"How so?" Hunter asked, but inside he knew exactly what she was saying. Tyler was seeing a life without arguments, without cold shoulders, without truth.

"Well, if we really were living together for more than Tyler's sake," she began hesitantly, "you and I would be acting differently toward each other." She paused, caught his gaze. "We'd be doing things."

While he was thinking about arguments and disagreement, she was talking about kissing, touching, gestures of affection and words of love. He could see it in her eyes. He could almost feel the hope pouring out of her, and for the first time since he officially moved in, Hunter felt a stab of guilt.

He ran his hand across his mouth, then drew a long breath. He hadn't forgotten that she was a dreamer. But he had thought that seven years of financial problems and loneliness had tempered her thoughts on life and love enough that when he dangled the more practical, more sensible reasons for getting married, she would see that fairy-tale love for exactly what it was: fiction.

"Yeah, we would probably argue more," he suggested lightly, trying to subtly show her his side of the story, as he shifted away from her.

"Maybe," she agreed, catching his hand when he attempted to inch away again. "But that's not bad if it's honest. And maybe we would also show him some good things, too."

"There are no good things," Hunter said quickly, without thinking, and from the stricken look on her face he knew he had hurt her. "Damn it, Abby, stop looking at me like that," he said and sprang from the swing. "I know firsthand that marriage isn't the joyous union that you and I had imagined when we were kids. It's true we would give Tyler a lot of security but if you're suggesting what I think you're suggesting, I can't let you go into this blindly." *Damn it anyway!* He growled in his head as he paced her porch. Why couldn't he just let her go into this blindly? No one had warned him.

He halted his internal tirade by reminding himself

this was Abby and he couldn't deliberately hurt her.
"All right, Abby, I have to be honest. Marriage is not
what you think it is."

She stared at him. "And you know this firsthand?"

Her question not only stopped his pacing, it startled
him. "You didn't know I was married?"

She straightened on the swing. "No. I didn't
know."

"Oh, shoot!" he said, then combed his fingers
through his hair. "Abby, sweetheart," he said soothingly as he sat beside her on the swing again. "It's
been seven years. I haven't been celibate and I haven't
even necessarily been good."

Abby got even stiffer. "I see."

"Aw, darn it!" he said, running his fingers through
his hair again. "I don't think you do see." This time
he caught her gaze. "I don't think you *can* see," he
said, getting angry now because she made him feel
like the scum of the earth. "I left here alone, broke,
mad at the world. At first, I started dating because I
needed company, then I worked around, got my bearings and eventually started my own business."

"That doesn't sound too bad."

"No, that part isn't. But what you don't know is
that a lot of times a different kind of woman comes
along with money."

"Oh."

He shoved his hands through his hair again. "Stop
it, all right? I wasn't that bad."

"I never said you were."

"And I didn't marry one of the women who threw
herself at me because I was rich. I married a woman
I worked with, the woman who had literally helped
me build the company. That was why she had more

than a leg to stand on when she took me to court to get the company when we divorced. I loved her...I loved her even after she slept with the site foreman and sued me for everything I worked for...."

The more Hunter tried to comfort Abby with his explanation, the more he hurt her. It would have been easier to handle thinking that he had married one of the women who threw herself at him. To think he had fallen in love, while she was at home, raising his child, wishing for him to come home, was almost too much to bear.

"Do you love her now?" she asked quietly.

Hunter sighed. "No. First of all, if it hadn't been for Grant Brewster investing in what was left of my company, she would have ruined me. Second, though I loved the sexual side of passion, I hated the fighting that came with it."

"Fighting isn't part of passion."

Hunter laughed. "Guess again."

"And that's why you always hold something of yourself in reserve?" Abby asked, her heart splintering into a million pieces. He had loved somebody else. He had been *passionate* with that other person. And now he was nothing. He was rich, friendly, honest, compassionate and even genuine, but he would never be passionate again.

He would never love again.

"That's why you shouldn't trust me," Hunter said. "I had intended to continue to try to talk you into marrying me, but now that I've sort of spelled out my life, even I don't want you to get involved with me. I want you to stay away from me."

"Fine," she said, numb and so hurt she almost couldn't move, couldn't breathe.

"Do you want me to leave?"

She looked at him. "I don't know. You're good for Tyler." She paused, freezing out her own concerns, her own feelings, and considered what was best for her son, then said, "I think the bottom line of what we need to do is explain to Tyler that we have something of an unusual situation. Since it's clear we will never have a family in the conventional sense," she said, tiptoeing around the painful truth that she would never marry Hunter Wyman, never have his love, "I think it's important that Tyler understand what we do have."

"You think that would work?"

"It's not as if other parents don't do it," Abby said calmly, though her broken heart ached and all she wanted to do was run to her room and punch a pillow, or scream, or cry. "It's important for him to understand that even though we live together and can live together happily, we're not married and you and I have no intention of getting married."

Hunter drew a long breath. "Okay."

"Okay," Abby said, rising from the swing. She wondered how her legs were carrying her and was shocked that she made it the whole way to her room before she burst into tears.

Everything she had wanted for the past seven years hadn't been a daydream or a fairy tale—it had been a lie.

Chapter Seven

"So, the thing is, Tyler," Hunter said, finishing the short speech he had given to his son, though he was awkward, uncomfortable and guilt-ridden, "your mother and I are not married and we have no intention of getting married, but because we are your parents and because we both love you, both of us *want* to live with you."

He couldn't understand why Abby allowed him in her home and their son's life if it made her so unhappy. Because if the pain in her eyes was anything to go by Abby was definitely heartbroken and miserable. Yet, there she sat, generously allowing him to be Tyler's father without restriction. Knowing he was the cause of her sadness created an odd jumble of emotions inside him. But he ignored them, realistically recognizing there wasn't a damned thing he could do about them or the past.

"We just don't want you to get the wrong impression," Abby interjected, tapping Tyler's forearm to get his attention. The little boy turned his big gray eyes on her. "We don't want you to get your hopes up and think that something is going to happen that isn't going to happen."

At the clumsiness of her last statement, she grimaced, but Hunter sensed Tyler understood what she had said.

"Hunter is still going to live here?" the boy asked.

Abby nodded. Hunter said an emphatic, "Yes."

"And everything's going to stay like it is?"

Hunter nodded. Abby said, "Absolutely."

Tyler shrugged. "Okay," he said and slid off his chair. "I'm going outside to play with Jimmy."

"Jimmy Parker?" Hunter asked curiously, knowing this was the kid who had bullied Tyler only a few weeks before, but Abby said, "Are you sure you're okay with our situation and that you understand?"

Tyler shrugged again and indifferently said, "Yeah."

"Then, you can go," Abby said, rising from her seat at the kitchen table. Tyler scurried out the back door.

"Well, that went pretty good," Hunter said with a relieved breath of air.

"It was fine," Abby agreed, smiling tightly, as she untied her apron. Without another word, she began to walk out of the room.

Hunter stopped her. "Where are you going?"

"I'm going shopping with Claire this afternoon, but, really, Hunter, that's not your concern. The one thing you and I forgot to discuss last night was that from here on out I won't be asking your whereabouts and you shouldn't ask mine."

Though her last statement put him in his place, it at

least took the stricken look from her face. He nodded. "Okay," he said and watched her walk away.

He cursed his life, his past, and all the stupid mistakes he had made, but most of all he cursed Abby. And her parents. He knew that was where she had gotten her foolish fairy-tale notions about life. And he knew that was why they had never thought him good enough for their daughter.

The worst of it was, it seemed he had proven them right.

When Abby phoned and said she would be having dinner with Claire, Hunter made supper for himself and Tyler. By the time Abby returned after eight, he had not only helped Tyler with his homework, he also had bathed him and put him into pajamas.

"What's this?" Abby asked, removing her coat as she entered the family room.

"We're watching TV," Tyler said, which was good because Hunter wasn't sure he was talking to Abby anymore. After an entire day to think all this through, he had decided Abby was a goody-two-shoes. Though she had tried to rebel in high school, the rebellion never "took" and here she was a little mirror image of her mother. He was glad—*glad*—she didn't want anything to do with him. Because he sure as hell didn't want anything to do with her.

But when she phoned him the following afternoon at the job site and told him that the elementary school principal had called, demanding both Abby and Hunter meet with her in her office, Hunter forgot all about being angry with her. He jumped into his SUV and roared off the construction site, fully expecting a confrontation with Jimmy Parker's parents, and he was ready. He would not let Abby face this alone. He would stand by her, he thought, expecting Abby to be in tears when he got to the school.

Instead, he found a calm sedate Abby sitting in the wooden captain's chair along the wall of the outer office waiting for him, and no Parkers anywhere in sight.

When he entered, she rose and primly said, "Mrs. McClosky said we could come in as soon as you arrived."

"Any idea what this is about?"

"Tyler's math grade is slipping," she quietly reported as she led Hunter to the closed door of Mrs. McClosky's office. "I'm guessing she wants to know why."

Hunter heard the insinuation in her cool voice that he was somehow behind the sliding grade since he was now the primary person helping Tyler with his homework, and he felt his blood pressure start to rise. But before he could say a word to defend himself, Abby opened the door and walked inside the principal's office.

"Mrs. McClosky," she greeted warmly, reaching across the desk to squeeze the old woman's hand. With that gesture, Hunter remembered Mrs. McClosky lived near enough to Abby that they considered themselves neighbors.

"Abigail," Mrs. McClosky replied, returning the hand squeeze. Then she looked over the rim of her luminescent reading glasses at Hunter. "Hunter," she said frostily.

Great. Now that he remembered Mrs. McClosky and Abby had lived in the same general vicinity virtually all their lives, he knew for sure he was going to get the rap for the math grade.

Mrs. McClosky invited them to sit with a wave of

her wrinkled hand and then sat in her old wooden chair behind the desk, smoothing her floral dress as she sat. "I called you in here today because I had some distressing news from Tyler's teacher."

"Look, if it's about the math grade," Hunter began. But Mrs. McClosky stopped him with one of those looks over the rim of her glasses again.

"Mr. Wyman," she said sternly. "This is not about something as simple as a math grade. Tyler has been bragging to the children in his class that he now lives with his father. Even I've seen your vehicle in Abby's driveway, but I didn't know with certainty that you were Tyler's father."

Though it had taken Hunter a few minutes and two near reprimands from Mrs. McClosky, with that comment he remembered that she was such a fussy old busybody that everybody called her Battle-ax McClosky.

"Yes, Hunter is Tyler's father," Abby said, "And he now lives with us."

"That's nice," Mrs. McClosky said, stretching the two words out until they could have been seven. "Lovely," she added through gritted teeth, her disapproval so obvious and so apparent Hunter almost slid down in his chair. "Unfortunately, Tyler is also bragging that his parents aren't married."

Honest Abby cleared her throat. "We're not."

"Wonderful," Mrs. McClosky said. "But what's upsetting his class is that Tyler's also bragging that his parents have no intention of getting married."

"The thing is, Mrs. McClosky..." Hunter began. But Mrs. McClosky again interrupted him.

"No. The thing is, Mr. Wyman, what you're doing is shameful and irresponsible. Worse, you have no qualms about exposing your immorality to Tyler. Frankly, I simply will not tolerate it."

Flabbergasted that the elementary school principal—who doubled as the town's head gossip—believed she had the right to pass judgment, Hunter couldn't even speak. But he didn't have to.

"You won't tolerate what?" Abby asked, and burst from her chair. "You won't tolerate the fact that I believe my son has a right to know his father, or that I run the only bed-and-breakfast in town and Mr. Wyman is a paying guest? On the day it becomes shameful and irresponsible to put food on the table for myself and my son, then I will stop working everywhere. Until then, Mrs. McClosky, you had better gather the facts before you start slinging accusations."

Furious, she strode to the door, but stopped halfway and faced the aghast principal again. "If you would have paid attention to what Tyler was saying, you would have understood that Mr. Wyman and I don't have a romantic relationship. *That's* why we're not getting married."

With a quick pivot, she opened the door and slammed it closed behind her, causing the glass to shimmer and jingle. Hunter winced, but when he faced Mrs. McClosky and saw she was sputtering with indignation, he swallowed back another laugh.

"Well, there's a side of Abby we don't get to see often, right, Mrs. M?"

"She shouldn't have shouted."

"You're lucky she didn't punch you," Hunter said, rising from his seat. "Just for the record and so that you have two official testimonies here, I'm Tyler's father but I'm only at the bed-and-breakfast as a guest, nothing more, and I think Abby is right. Instead of spreading rumors, you should be responding to rumors with the truth."

"Well, now that I know the truth I will certainly do that," Mrs. McClosky said, trying to salvage her pride.

But Hunter only grinned. "Don't bother seeing me out. I'll find my own way," he said, then left the building with grace and dignity. Only when he was behind the closed door of his SUV did he burst into a full-scale belly laugh.

Instead of returning to the job site, he drove to the bed-and-breakfast, jumped out of his vehicle and ran up the walk. In three quick hops he was across the porch and into the kitchen, where he grabbed Abby by the waist and spun her around twice before lifting her above his head.

"You were so funny."

She slapped his shoulder. "Put me down," she said, then slapped him again.

"You should have seen the look on old Battle-ax McClosky's face."

Abby couldn't help it, her lips twitched, then she smiled, then she started to laugh. "That good, huh?"

"Fantastic."

"I didn't think you remembered our old nickname for her."

Hunter grinned. "In that particular office, with that particular old bat, a good many things came back to me this afternoon. But don't change the subject. You were priceless."

"I wasn't supposed to be priceless. I was furious."

"Anybody ever tell you you're beautiful when you're furious?"

He had. Lots and lots and lots of times. In fact, to Abby he sounded exactly the way he had when he said it all those years ago. Even his tone of voice was the same.

She wiggled in his hands until he put her down. "Actually, yes," she said, walking away from him.

Though Hunter had been happy plenty of times since his return, this was the first time she had seen him natural and relaxed, and almost his old self. And the last place she needed to be was in his arms, being reminded of what things had been like between them seven years ago.

She busied herself with gathering ingredients to make dinner, but Hunter walked up behind her and turned her away from the counter.

His hands on her waist, he stared into her eyes. "I used to say that, didn't I?"

Almost overwhelmed from the combination of the confrontation with Mrs. McClosky, the return of the real Hunter Wyman, and his nearness, Abby only nodded.

"Because you got mad a lot when you were younger," he said softly, quietly, as if he were only remembering himself.

She nodded again.

"You were such a bad girl," he said, then he grinned. "I'll bet your mother had seven fits a day over you."

"She lived."

He conceded that with a nod of his head. "Is that why you're so quiet now, so good? Because being bad ended up hurting you?"

She shrugged. "Maybe."

"Sometimes I think that's what happened to me, too."

For this, she looked up into his gray-green eyes. The

vulnerability she saw in them almost took her breath away. Of course. He had been hurt. For all his bravado about the cheating wife who nearly ended up with his company, the missing element he neglected to admit was that he had been hurt.

"Maybe that is what happened to you, too," she agreed softly.

"We're a pair, aren't we?" he asked, then without warning, without permission, he bent his head and kissed her.

And Abby let herself fall into the kiss, but not as far, not as passionately as she had his first two kisses, and he slowly pulled away.

"Now we not only have a promise to each other to keep this relationship platonic," he said, backing away from her. "We also have a promise to an elementary school principal who could start spying on us with binoculars since you embarrassed her by yelling at her. Neither one of us wants Tyler to be the object of rumors and since we now know Gwen McClosky is watching, I guess we'd better see to it that everything between us really does stay platonic."

She gave him a rueful smile and nodded, but she didn't agree because of the gossip or even because of Tyler. Truth be known, she wasn't even agreeing out of concern for herself. From the expression in Hunter's eyes, she could see that the relationship that he so easily dismissed as nothing but a scandal had hurt him a great deal more than he let on. He would have a sexual relationship with her, or even a marriage of convenience, but he couldn't have an intimate, passionate relationship like the one they had before because his last intimate, passionate relationship had devastated him.

* * *

"So the thing is, Tyler…" Hunter paused, looking to Abby for help, but she only motioned for him to continue with a wave of her hand. "It is true that I stay here with you and it's also true that I stay here partially because you are here. But I also stay here because your mother runs a bed-and-breakfast—like a hotel—and I don't have anywhere else to stay because I'm not from around here…."

He turned pleading eyes on Abby and Abby caught Tyler's attention by tapping the back of his hand. "What Hunter is saying is that he is a guest here like any of the other people who stay here. And that's the biggest reason he lives with us. Not only because he's your father."

Tyler looked from Hunter to Abby and then back to Hunter again. "You don't live here because you're my dad?"

"Well, yes…but there are also other reasons," Hunter explained. "But that isn't really the point. The truth is, Tyler, you can't go around telling people that your parents live together but aren't married. It's a big, ugly, complicated adult thing…sort of a paranoia for some people like Mrs. McClosky, and it could get us into trouble."

Tyler considered that. "Oh."

"Not big trouble," Abby assured, tapping his hand again. "Little trouble. But it's just the kind of thing you don't talk about because our situation is different."

"How come you don't want to get married?" he asked, looking from Abby to Hunter and back to Abby again. Abby swallowed hard. She should have been expecting this but she wasn't.

Hunter, however, came to her rescue.

"It's like this, Tyler," Hunter said quietly, gently. "I think a great deal of your mother, but I haven't seen her in seven years, so I really don't know her anymore." He paused, caught Abby's gaze and then said, "I think your mother also has a lot of respect for me, but she doesn't really know me anymore, either."

"So, when you get to know each other you could get married?"

"We could," Hunter agreed, fielding the question before Abby had a chance. "But other things happened. For one, your mom has spent the past seven years taking care of you. Even you told me that she didn't get to go out much."

Tyler shook his head.

"So," Hunter said with a short chuckle, "she might not want to marry me. She might want to have some fun first."

Tyler gave Abby a horrified look and Hunter brought his attention back to him again. "For another thing, though, Tyler, I have to tell you that I was married before and I just don't think I really want to get married again."

"Did you get divorced?"

Hunter nodded. "I'm divorced."

"Devon Malcom's parents are divorced."

"Lots of people get divorced."

"But Devon's mom has a new husband and his dad has a new wife."

"And I'll bet he gets lots of stuff for Christmas, and four presents for his birthday, which is good. But that's not what's going to happen here, with us," Hunter said, hoisting Tyler from the chair and into his arms for a quick hug before he put him on the floor.

"Why don't you go start your bath and then I'll come up and read to you from a comic book."

"All right!" Tyler said. His attention sufficiently diverted, he darted from the room.

"That was cheating."

Hunter smiled. "No, that was getting everybody out of a conversation that none of us was really ready for. The kid is six. There is no possible way he could understand that some people aren't cut out to be married or that some marriages only make situations worse."

"I suppose you're right," Abby agreed, rising from her seat. "You go ahead upstairs. I'll take care of the dishes."

"You sure?"

"Hey, you've got a comic book to read."

Hunter grinned. "I know."

"Oh, you dog. You're going to enjoy this more than he is."

Hunter's grin grew. "I know."

With that he left Abby alone in her kitchen and though she felt satisfied about their conversation with Tyler, other things began jumping into her memory. Like the fact that Hunter's mother had left his father when Hunter was only a baby. And the fact that Hunter was raised by an alcoholic father who didn't necessarily abuse him, but who definitely ignored him.

It seemed that in all the hustle and bustle of sorting through the seven years that had passed, they had forgotten that the preceding twenty-four hadn't been all peaches and cream for him, either. But now that she was remembering these things, Abby finally saw that one bad marriage hadn't spoiled Hunter. Two bad marriages had. The one he lived and the one that produced him.

It was no wonder he was sour on marriage and no wonder he was sure he would never change his mind. It was easy to see why living alone, maybe even being lonely, was more appealing to him than risking another painful marriage.

Chapter Eight

Coincidentally, Mrs. McClosky was the first person they saw when they stepped into the church hall for St. Bernadine's annual paprika chicken and dumplings dinner that Sunday afternoon.

"Abigail. Hunter," she said, nodding stiffly at both as she took their tickets. She turned her gaze to Tyler. "And you, young man, I hope you're doing something about that math grade."

"Yes, ma'am," he said, ducking his head.

"It's nice to see you, too, Gwen," Hunter said, then maneuvered Abby and Tyler away from the ticket window and to Mrs. Kollar who was seating the dinner patrons.

"You called her Gwen!" Tyler said with a giggle.

"That's her name," Hunter responded easily, but Abby could see he was hiding a smirk.

"Can I call her Gwen?" Tyler asked.

"No," Abby said at the same time that Hunter said, "When you get older."

"This is one of those respect issues, Tyler," Abby said, as she, Hunter and Tyler were directed to the next three empty folding chairs at one of the long paper-covered tables. "Because Mrs. McClosky is in a position of authority in your life, you call her Mrs. McClosky...and not Gwen," she added, giving Hunter a pointed look. "When you get older and she's not one of your authority figures, you may call her Gwen."

"Why don't you call her Gwen?" Tyler asked innocently.

"Because I—"

"Because your mother is a chicken," Hunter supplied, displaying the platter of chicken that had been passed to him. "She's still afraid of Mrs. McClosky."

"I'm not afraid of Mrs. McClosky."

"Then why don't you call her Gwen?" Hunter asked, catching her gaze as if daring her to contradict him.

"I don't call her Gwen because I respect her."

"I respect her," Hunter quickly countered. "Some days I even sort of like her. I think that's why I feel comfortable enough to use her first name. I don't have her up on a pedestal. To me she's just a person."

Abby would have liked to remind Hunter that she had only a few days before yelled at Mrs. McClosky, unequivocally proving that she wasn't a chicken. Lately, he had been teasing her so much and so often that at least three times a day she found herself getting into silly, pretend arguments with him over stupid things until they were laughing like two nuts. But considering that they were in public, and with Tyler present, she said nothing, only placed food on her plate as the dishes were handed to her.

They talked about inconsequential things while they ate, but after they left the table to peruse the small booths of baked goods and crafts being offered for sale, Abby didn't get much of a chance to speak with Hunter or her son again.

Hunter might have only returned to Brewster County a few weeks before, but he had already renewed many acquaintances. More than that, though, he was one of the two people putting in the new mall. He was a source of jobs. He was an important person. If he stayed around long enough, he would become a community leader. Everybody knew that. And everybody wanted to shower him with respect, admiration and affection of sorts while there was still time to get in his good graces.

As she strolled from booth to booth, examining the wares, Abby fully expected Hunter to ship Tyler back to her since having a six-year-old at his side could definitely put a crimp in conversation. But through the hour-long stay, Hunter never once appeared even slightly uneasy with Tyler hanging on his arm. In fact, the little boy looked as if he belonged at Hunter's side. Not just because Tyler was happy, but also because Hunter was competent, confident and even content having Tyler climb up his side, hide behind him and nearly use him as a jungle gym.

"Find everything you want?" Hunter asked, grinning as he looked at her odd assortment of purchases.

"Just about," Abby said, then she winced. "Come on, Hunter, who can resist a ceramic pig refrigerator magnet?"

"Especially in magenta," Hunter teased, taking the little pig from her hand and examining it. "It'll be a lovely addition to your green and yellow kitchen."

"I bought it for contrast," she said, then she faced Tyler. "I also bought you a comic book holder."

"Cool!" Tyler grabbed the wooden three-tiered object that was really nothing more than a spray-painted frame with fabric pouches.

"This is certainly interesting," Hunter said, inspecting the thing, and Abby almost winced again. She didn't really know if it was supposed to be a comic book holder, but it would work as one.

"I'm going to show my friends!" Tyler said, then raced away, straight to Jimmy Parker.

"They're friends, they aren't friends, they're friends, they aren't friends," Hunter said, his gaze following the trip their son had just made. "What's the deal with this?"

"They're six," Abby reminded him. "Can't you remember being six?"

"Actually, I can," Hunter said distantly, turning away from her, ostensibly to look at Tyler. But Abby squeezed her eyes shut knowing she had just reminded Hunter of something he didn't want to remember. Especially on a day when he was being treated with such obvious respect and admiration by the town, which hadn't as much as whispered a word of objection when he left seven years before.

As quickly and artfully as possible, she changed the subject. "There are more ceramic pigs over there if you want one," she said, taking Hunter's elbow and pointing him toward the bright booth.

Hunter burst out laughing. "What would I want with a ceramic pig?"

"You could put it by mine on the refrigerator."

She hadn't intended anything by the comment, but

from the way Hunter studied her she knew he had taken some kind of meaning from what she had said.

He smiled. "Are you sure Gwen would approve? First, we're living together, now you'd like to see my pig on your refrigerator."

Abby sighed. "I didn't mean anything by that."

"I know," Hunter said, but he stroked one finger down her cheek. "It's a nice thought, though, us having side-by-side things."

"Yeah, like twin beds," Abby said, pulling herself away from him because he was just too seductive. He could take the simplest, stupidest comment or idea and transform it into a way to flirt with her. It was borderline annoying and on the road to habitual that he continually saw them in a role neither one of them wanted…. She stopped her thoughts.

Habitual. Flirting with her was becoming a habit for Hunter. Habits were instinct. Instinct was what came naturally. Whether he knew it or not, his feelings were changing. How he saw her was changing. Maybe even how he saw relationships was changing.

She pivoted to face him again. By this time, however, Hunter was involved in another conversation. But Abby decided that was good. She wasn't sure she wanted to share this with him. She wasn't sure she wanted to share it with anybody because it was too new, too unexplored to share.

Because the bottom line she saw was that Hunter was changing. Not only had he easily slid into the role of father for Tyler, but also, he was growing comfortable with her. And the more comfortable he grew, the more he would trust her and the more he trusted her, the more he would see that she wasn't like his mother or his first wife.

She had missed the obvious. All Hunter needed was time, consistency and affection and he would be able to love her. No, she realized. All he needed was time, consistency and some kind of sign from her and he would be able to admit he loved her. Because the truth, suddenly so clear before her, was that he already loved her.

Her breath caught in her throat. *He loved her.* The feeling was so warm and wonderful she could have wrapped it around her like a thick coat. But before that thought fully gelled in her brain, she had another, equally shocking thought. She loved him, too. She loved the new, modified, mature, stately, almost regal Hunter. Otherwise, the knowledge that he loved her wouldn't be so incredibly intoxicating.

Tyler spun away from Jimmy Parker and bounded toward her, but Hunter scooped him up, twirled him around once and then set him on his feet. "No running in the hall," he scolded, but sweetly, and Abby's heart stopped.

She couldn't believe she hadn't seen this sooner. Not only had Hunter slipped by her defenses simply by being himself, but she'd slipped by his. All she had to do was let things happen at their own pace and everything would work out.

Hunter spent the rest of the afternoon with Grant, going over blueprints, specifications and the contract for the structural steel, and Tyler went to play with his friends, so Abby was alone in the big house, trying not to be nervous, trying not to let the ramifications of all her discoveries get the better of her. To keep her mind off things, she baked cupcakes and when Hunter and Tyler entered through the back door at the same time, both stopped dead in their tracks.

"You baked," Hunter said, attempting to sound enthusiastic, but sounding only dismayed.

"Cupcakes," Tyler said, equally uneasy.

"I used a box mix and canned icing," Abby said, and when both Hunter and Tyler breathed a sigh of relief, she tossed her dish towel to the counter. "That's it. No more food for either one of you."

"Aw, come on, Abby," Hunter said, following after her as she bounded out of the room. "We've been patient."

"My cooking isn't that bad."

"Your cooking is fine," Hunter happily announced. "It's your baking that scares the life out of us."

"Oh, gee, thanks," Abby said as Hunter caught her and spun her around. "That makes me feel much better."

"Hey, neither one of us wants to insult you, but we've discussed this and we'd like the option to refuse to pretend that things you bake taste good when they don't. In fact," he said, gentling his voice, "Tyler and I agree that pretending we like your pastries won't help you to get any better. If you're going to learn how to bake, you need to know how to take the bad news so you can improve."

Abby couldn't help it, she burst out laughing. "I'm not that bad."

"Yes, you are," Hunter insisted kindly, but firmly. "Everything you bake tastes like it has too much baking soda in it or maybe too much salt. Don't you follow recipes?"

"Well, yes, but I try to spiff them up by adding extra stuff. Corky does it all the time at the diner."

"Corky is also close to eighty. He has at least sixty years of experience on you. Come on, give your boys a break. Until you have another thirty years of baking under your belt, stick with exactly what the recipe says.''

Abby nodded congenially, but inside she felt the warm, mushy feeling she had gotten at the paprika chicken and dumplings dinner. He loved her. He just didn't know it yet.

''Well, the cupcakes are from a box, and I have soup and toasted cheese sandwiches ready to cook for supper.''

''Great, fine,'' Hunter said and followed her into the kitchen. But his intuition was screaming that something was wrong. Abby should have kicked and hissed and spit when he told her how much he and Tyler hated her baking. Instead, she didn't merely take it gracefully, she seemed happy about it.

He covertly watched her the entire way through dinner. She didn't seem unhappy or at all upset over his criticism, so Hunter decided to chalk the whole thing up to changes in her that had occurred in the years he was away. And he had to admit he liked the mature version of Abby, but lately, especially since she'd yelled at Mrs. McClosky, he had really been missing the little spitfire she had been.

But, Hunter realized, Abby hadn't been a spitfire so much in public as she had been in private. He loved the way she had always been able to handle herself— and him—when they were around other people. And when he remembered that, Hunter realized that what he was missing about Abby was the personal, physical relationship they shared.

He felt it again, after they had put Tyler to bed and she invited him downstairs for a cup of tea. It wasn't the first time they had shared private minutes together in the evening, but it was the first time she sat beside him on the sofa. She asked about his day. He told her that reviewing specifications with Grant didn't make for interesting evening conversation. Then all of a sudden she was in his arms and he was kissing her. Just like he would have kissed her seven years ago. And she was responding, exactly how she would have responded seven years ago. All wonderful abandon and fire, somehow wrapped in a warm cocoon of love.

When he named the emotion, he jerked away and bounced from the sofa. "Don't!" he said, then squeezed his eyes shut. All the lines kept getting blurred. Feelings were leaking into things that should have been nothing but fun. And he didn't want that. Not now, not ever.

Though his heart was beating wildly and his mind was filling with thoughts that paralyzed him, Abby appeared perfectly calm.

"Hunter, relax," she said sweetly, then patted the couch cushion beside her.

He only stared at her until he figured out that she was innocent enough that she genuinely believed all these feelings were right and good and would lead to a bright future. Frustrated, he ran his hand across his mouth. As if it wasn't bad enough he had to control himself, now he was being put into the position of having to keep her in line, too.

Frustration mixed with anger and when he spoke, his words came out sharper than he intended. "I not only know that we've discussed all this before, I also know that I warned you about me."

She smiled at him. "I'm not worried about you."

He caught her chin between his thumb and index finger and lifted her face until she looked at him.

"You should be," he said succinctly. "Because I have no intention of changing. I do not want what you want. And if you're smart you won't want what I want."

With that he stormed out of the living room. Cursing himself, cursing her for being so trusting and cursing life for dangling very good things in front of two people who didn't deserve to be hurt or disappointed any more than they already had been.

Chapter Nine

"**W**ell, what have we got here?"

Grant Brewster asked the question as Hunter hoisted
Tyler up the makeshift steps of the construction trailer
that served as an office on the site of the new mall.

"It's only me, Grant," Tyler said, getting his foot-
ing on the slanted floor.

"I see that," Grant said, smiling. "It's just that I
wasn't here the other Saturday you came with your
father, so I've never seen you out here before." He
scratched his chin. "Come to think of it, I've never
seen you anywhere without your mother."

"She didn't want to come," Tyler advised seriously.

"That's because this is man stuff," Grant said, lifting Tyler to one of the tall stools beside a drafting
table.

"Oh, Lord," Hunter groaned. "Don't let Abby hear
you say that. She would kill you for putting sexist
ideas in his head."

Grant laughed. "That's our Abby. Still as feisty as ever."

At the mention of Abby and feistiness, heat and need poured through Hunter and he remembered their kisses from the Sunday before. His knees actually became weak simply from the memory, but he squelched the instant reaction by reminding himself that he and Abby wanted two different things. He had tried being married and he knew what marriage did to people. He wouldn't go into it again. At least not dishonestly. If Abby could marry him for sensible reasons like Tyler, money and sex, Hunter would have her in front of a preacher tomorrow. Since she wanted love and bliss and things that didn't exist, things that actually made people miserable trying to create them, he planned to stay away from her.

He faced Grant. "So what's on tap for today?"

"Since it's Saturday, I figure that we should both get out of here at a decent hour."

"Agreed," Hunter said, casting a quick glance at his six-year-old son who appeared to be happily exploring everything and anything on the drafting table, including the contents of old coffee cups.

"So, let's just see if we can't write the remainder of the request for bids for the masonry."

"Good enough," Hunter said, but before he sat down, he found a clean legal pad and some markers used for color coding blueprints and handed them to Tyler. "Think you can entertain yourself for about two hours?"

Tyler looked up at Hunter and smiled. The sweet look he gave was so compelling that Hunter felt his chest expand with love. "Sure," he said simply, taking the supplies from Hunter's hands.

Hunter swallowed hard and took his seat behind one of the two old desks that sat across from each other at the rear of the trailer. For the next hour he read—or tried to read—the specifications for the masonry, but his eyes kept straying to Tyler and so did his thoughts.

He was unexpectedly thrilled to be a father, but more than that, he was incredibly proud of Tyler. Abby had done an amazing job of raising him. He was bright and polite, energetic and mischievous, but also thoughtful and caring. A father couldn't ask for a better son and Hunter had gotten his with very little effort. And the effort he had put in had been nothing but pure joy. He always realized he owed Abby a huge debt of gratitude, but today it was more obvious than ever. And more insistently pounding in his brain that though he couldn't pay her back the way he knew she wanted to be repaid—with real love—there had to be some way he could repay her.

When Grant rose to leave, Hunter sheepishly peered at the page of notes he had scribbled, comparing them to Grant's six computer-generated pages.

"You can make up for it Monday," Grant said as he locked the door behind them. He took a quick glance at Tyler who stood well behaved at Hunter's side, then looked at Hunter. "Maybe what you need to do is a little bonding."

"We live together," Hunter reminded Grant.

"I know," Grant said. "But living together is ordinary. My brothers and I all discovered that it sometimes takes doing something out of the ordinary to really get to know somebody."

Deciding Grant was right, Hunter led Tyler to his SUV and after buckling his seat belt said, "We have a few hours before your mom expects us home. What would you like to do?''

Tyler lifted his big gray-green eyes to Hunter and Hunter was again struck with the wonder of being a parent. When Tyler grinned, Hunter's heart swelled with love.

"Can we do anything I want?" he asked innocently.

Hunter smiled indulgently. "Absolutely anything," he said, praying the kid would come up with something within reason.

"Good, then I want to buy my mom a birthday present."

Hunter remembered that Abby's birthday was in two days. He probably wouldn't have made the connection if Tyler hadn't said something, but now that Tyler brought it up, Hunter remembered it, too. He also realized that this was one of those silent, yet effective ways he could thank Abby for raising Tyler so well.

"You got it," Hunter agreed. He drove them to the shopping mall in a nearby town, the mall which would be the competition for his and Grant's mall. Tyler virtually dragged him to a women's clothing store.

"There," he said, pointing at a dress on a mannequin. Red and sequined, it didn't look like anything for which Abby would have use.

He cleared his throat. "That's nice," he said, not wanting to insult Tyler. "But what do you say we go inside and see if we can't find something that she could wear somewhere like church."

"She could wear that one to church," Tyler insisted, again pointing at the red sequined tank dress which reminded Hunter of the streetwalkers he had seen in Philadelphia when he visited Chas Brewster a few years back.

"She could," Hunter agreed, guiding his son into the store. "But I think she would probably like this one better," he said, grabbing a simple blue and white dress being used as a display.

"That's okay," Tyler reluctantly said. "But so is this one." He reached for a pink sheath that was only one step less gaudy than the red sequined number. But because it actually was less gaudy and because Hunter recognized Tyler wanted to be a part of the choosing process he agreed to buy that dress, too.

After discussions with the salesclerk that resulted in a good estimate of Abby's proper size and another trip through the store that resulted in the purchase of two dresses, three shirts, two summer-weight sweaters, two skirts, four pairs of slacks and a handful of hair ornaments, Tyler seemed satisfied. Hunter knew that the gift was extravagant and that Abby might even be annoyed, but there were two things at work here. First, he didn't want to deny Tyler this chance to get his mother a gift. Second, Hunter himself felt like rewarding—even spoiling—Abby for all the sacrifices she had made in raising their son.

He believed they had done a damned fine job with their birthday purchases and even began to plan how they could create something of a surprise party—or at the very least get a cake from the bakery—when Hunter realized Tyler sat huddled in the seat beside him, his arms crossed over his chest, his lower lip hanging down as if he were in abject misery.

"Hey, kid, we just spent almost five hundred dollars on your mother's birthday, so why the long face?"

"We didn't get her what she really wants."

Hunter almost wrecked his SUV when he brought it to a screeching halt. After two hours in a woman's clothing store, the last thing he wanted to do was return all this stuff and start over again. "What was all that about back there in the store if we didn't get your mother what she really wants?"

"Oh, she's gonna like the clothes, but what she really needs is a car."

Hunter breathed a huge sigh of relief and pulled his gearshift out of Park and into Drive again. "That's normal, Tyler. Everybody would like to have a new car."

"Yeah, I know," Tyler said, raising his gaze to his father's. Then he grinned. "Heck, I'd like a new car and I can't even drive."

The silliness of his comment made Hunter laugh, but more than that, the sheer joy of being with his son overcame him. For a good ten minutes he actually thought about buying Abby a car if only to see how happy it would make Tyler, but dismissed the idea because he realized that with only the slightest push he could spoil his son. He also realized that Abby was a proud woman who might not like the idea that Hunter had bought her so many things. And when he wrapped the gifts, he decided to make it look as if Tyler had bought all of them, and even went to the jewelry shop in town and bought Abby a single gold chain from himself.

Two days later, as she opened present after present from Tyler, Tyler danced around the dining room table with glee. Hunter sat back on his chair and simply enjoyed the scene. He had never seen anyone so happy to give as Tyler was and again Hunter was struck by the notion of how much Abby had sacrificed to raise his son. For Tyler to be so thrilled to see her get a few items of clothing, he must have watched her do without even bare necessities. Though Abby tried to temper her reaction, she couldn't hide the fact that she loved the clothes any more than she could hide the fact that she knew exactly how Tyler had purchased them.

When she sent Tyler out to the kitchen to get her a glass of water, Hunter pretty much knew what was coming.

"You shouldn't have," she hissed in a whisper.

Hunter shrugged, then grinned. "I couldn't help it. He was thrilled to do this."

"I know that," Abby said, obviously struggling to be sensible and calm. "But don't you realize that I can't refuse any of this or take any of it back because if I do I will hurt his feelings?"

"Oh, well," Hunter said with a shrug, then forked a bite of cake to ignore her.

"I have to pay you back for this," she insisted quickly, recognizing that Tyler would be returning soon with her water.

"Great. Bake me some cupcakes," he said, then he burst out laughing.

Tyler entered the room sloshing water over the sides of a sturdy tumbler. "Here, Mom."

"Thank you, sweetheart," Abby said, smiling at Tyler before glaring at Hunter the very second her son looked away.

Hunter successfully avoided any further argument or abuse from her until after Tyler was in bed. She found him on the back porch swing, sat beside him and without preamble said, "I have to reimburse you for part of that."

Hunter groaned. "Oh, for Pete's sake, Abby, I owe you six years of back child support. You can't possibly compare a few sweaters to that. Six years," he said emphatically, again overwhelmed by how much she'd done, how long she had struggled. "By the way, has Chas come up with any numbers for me on that yet?"

Abby cleared her throat. "Yeah. I have his figures of what the minimum would have been and then another set of figures of what you should have paid based upon your income."

"Ouch," Hunter said, wincing. "Do you have an investment counselor?"

"Yeah, right," Abby said, then lightly slapped his arm as a reprimand for teasing her.

"I'm not kidding, Abby. You're going to do okay with this."

She looked at him. "You just don't get it, do you?"

"Get what?"

"I don't want your money. Having you here and having you help with Tyler is enough. You pay for groceries, you pay to stay at the bed-and-breakfast, you give Tyler money, you've bought him clothes. You even helped him buy me birthday presents. Those are the kinds of things a father does. That's what I want Tyler to see. I don't want him to see himself as some sort of commodity that I get paid money for."

"So we won't tell him."

"We won't have to tell him. He'll pick up on it from conversation."

Hunter stared at her. "What are you saying? You don't want the back child support?"

She shook her head. "If you want to put money in a college fund for Tyler that would be great. But I don't want you giving me some sort of lump sum check. I don't want it and I don't think Tyler would understand it." She paused and drew a long breath. "Start a college fund and everybody will be happy."

Hunter was about to tell her that he didn't feel right about that because it was Abby who had suffered, not Tyler. Though Tyler might not have had brand names, Hunter couldn't imagine that his son had done without anything in his young life, though he could see that Abby had given up everything. Establishing a college fund was something like paying the baby instead of the baby-sitter and it didn't sit right with him. Besides, providing Tyler with a good education was something Hunter had planned to do anyway.

At the same time, he knew better than to argue. Abby wasn't so much wearing her I've-made-up-my-mind-so-don't-argue-with-me expression, as she was soft and vulnerable and he felt that if he argued with her, he would hurt her somehow.

He had spent Tyler's entire lifetime hurting her. He refused to do it anymore. Even when arguing with her would be for her own good. Instead, he put his arm around her and pulled her to him. He wasn't surprised when she nestled into his side as if seeking comfort.

"We had some weekend," he said quietly.

"I'll bet you did."

"He's such a great kid, Abby," Hunter said, glad he wasn't facing her because tears actually filled his eyes. "You've given me such a great gift with him."

Abby laughed unexpectedly. "That's funny. That's exactly what I used to think about you. That you had given me such a great gift in Tyler."

"Didn't you think it was odd that I didn't care about my own son?"

She shrugged. "Yes. But I simply decided you didn't know what you were missing."

"You gave me the benefit of the doubt?"

She smiled against his shoulder. "Something like that."

No one had ever had the reservoir of patience and faith in him that Abby had and, again, Hunter was overcome with emotion. He reached down and took her chin in his two fingers so he could tip her face up to his.

Then against his own better judgment he kissed her. She kissed him back but she also pulled away. Slowly, as if tempted to continue, but common sense won over impulse. She shifted away from him, then quickly rose from the swing.

"Good night, Hunter," she said as she walked to the screen door and then slipped into the kitchen.

Hunter cursed. Not because she left him but because of why she left him. What she wanted from him was something he couldn't give and it angered him that she made him feel inadequate. But, at the same time, he also owed her and he couldn't silence that nagging voice that kept insisting to him that he was hurting this good and decent woman, and he had to make it up to her.

He couldn't do anything about the fact that he had been gone when she had their child. He couldn't do anything about the fact that he refused to give his heart away completely. But he could most certainly do something about the money.

"Cover your eyes."

Abby stared at Hunter as if he were crazy, but Tyler's gaze shot from his book to Hunter. Eager and perceptive, he said, "Why do you want Mom to cover her eyes?"

"I bought her something."

Tyler came to full alert.

"You better not have," Abby said, her voice dripping with warning.

"Hey, you don't want back child support. Chas tells me you told him that as long as I'm staying at the bed-and-breakfast helping you, you won't even take present child support. I had to do something."

Abby stared at him. "You're doing plenty."

"Well, now I've just done a little more," he said and directed her toward the back door. Standing in front of her, blocking her view, he led her across the porch and down the steps, then he shifted out of her way, revealing the brand-new candy-apple red convertible he had bought for her. "This is for you."

"Oh, my gosh," was all she could say. She clasped her hands over her mouth.

Tyler screamed. "Wow! Cool!"

Seemingly unable to resist, she ran her fingers over the smooth enticing metal.

"You like it?" Hunter asked quietly.

Tears filled Abby's eyes and she swallowed hard. "I love it. But I can't accept it."

Tyler wailed his displeasure, and Hunter groaned. "Oh, come on, Abby. You won't take anything from me."

She faced him then, tears perched precariously on the rim of her eyelids, her lips trembling. But when she spoke, it was to Tyler. "Tyler, honey, why don't you go see if Jimmy Parker can play for a while?"

"I want to ride in the car!"

She shook her head. "We'll talk about the car later.

For now go to the Parkers. Tell Mrs. Parker I'll be by to get you before dinner.''

"All right," Tyler said. Obviously disgusted, he stomped down the driveway beside the bed-and-breakfast to the front sidewalk that would lead him to the Parkers'.

"I take plenty from you," Abby told Hunter without preamble. Her eyes still glistened with tears, her lips still trembled when she spoke. "Whether you know it or not, we're creating something of a normal life for Tyler. When you do things like this," she said, waving her hand in the direction of the car, "you ruin it.''

"Ruin it! How?"

"You're giving him the impression that money handles everything.''

"No, I'm showing my son that he should be appreciative of the people in his life. And generous.''

"Are you sure you're not showing him that he can buy people off?''

At that Hunter cursed roundly. "I can't believe you won't let me help you.''

"You are helping me. And you're helping Tyler a great deal more than you're helping me, just by being around. Extravagant gestures like this," she said, her lips quaking, "don't help. Take it back.''

"All right. Fine. Whatever." He turned and pounded up the six steps of the back porch. "I'll get my coat and the keys and be out of your hair in two minutes.''

Abby slipped into the house behind him. While he went in search of his coat, she sneaked upstairs and locked herself in her bedroom where she finally let the tears fall.

He didn't see that he was trying to substitute gifts and toys and even money for love. All she wanted was his love and he couldn't give it. If she would have taken the car—and she was sorely tempted—it would have been like a signal to him that he could get around differences of opinion simply by buying gifts.

And the worst part of it was, she couldn't be angry with him, though she was furious with the woman who had hurt him so much that he didn't even trust Abby anymore. A surge of pain poured through her at the notion that Hunter had married someone else, and she knew that there was more behind their inability to trust each other than the pain he had suffered at another woman's hand. The very fact that he had married someone else, without thought for Abby, hurt her to the core.

The truth was they had seven years of their own mistrust and suspicions to overcome and they weren't going to have a decent relationship until they broke down and admitted that to each other.

In fact, if she pushed this logic to its limit, Abby was actually the first woman to hurt him. Albeit through her parents' lies. For seven years Hunter believed she deserted him. Hated him. Didn't want him around.

Was it any wonder he didn't trust her?

Chapter Ten

"So, the way I see this, these are the kinds of wounds only time can heal," Abby said as she served more coffee to Kristen, Claire and Lily. "He's not going to learn to trust me again without time for me to prove that I'm worthy of his trust," she continued unemotionally, hiding her pain because she didn't want to add to her misery by having people feel sorry for her.

Mrs. Romani, Kristen and Grant's housekeeper, was watching the triplets that morning and given this opportunity to really talk with her three friends, Abby had invited them to the bed-and-breakfast. They sat in her living room, sipping coffee, while Abby told her story. As she related the last of what had happened over the weekend, both Claire and Lily Brewster nodded their understanding and agreement.

But Kristen said, "Poppycock."

"Excuse me?" Abby said, almost choking on her coffee.

"Poppycock," Kristen said. "I think you're dead wrong. You have a man who is very interested in you, interested enough to buy you a car—a *car*," she repeated incredulously, "and you're going to send him off into the world of other women rather than try to help him to work through your past. I think you're nuts."

"Then what should I do?" Abby asked, eager to take anybody's suggestions because Hunter was as forlorn as she was. Her own suffering she could handle; his was killing her.

"If I were you I would propose," Kristen suggested flippantly. "I've been watching Hunter all these weeks and I think he needs security. I think that if the two of you were married, eventually he would grow comfortable enough to admit that the emotion behind all these gifts is love. In fact, I think that might have been the reason Hunter asked you to marry him when he first returned home. In his heart, I think the man knows he loves you. The problem is he's been burned. I don't blame him for being careful."

"Kristen, he's beyond careful. He's convinced himself love doesn't exist. It almost seems he believes that love is a trap for fools. So he won't let himself feel anything. The second I sense he's actually about to put his heart into something, I visibly see him pull back. I think that if I married him, he would never admit he loves me because he wouldn't have any motivation to change."

"Could be," Claire agreed thoughtfully, "but I'm starting to see Kristen's point. Think back to Hunter's childhood, Ab," she said. "His mother deserted his father, and his father might have stayed around to raise Hunter, but he virtually ignored him. You combine his past with the mess your parents made of your relationship, then add in his first marriage, and you might just get a man who won't change for anything—except security.''

"My point exactly," Kristen said proudly.

Abby drew a long breath. "Okay, I see what you're saying. I'm not sure I agree that I should ask him to marry me, but I see what you're saying."

Kristen shrugged. "You could always test the water."

"How?"

"I would start with a private dinner," Kristen said, thinking aloud. "If you say that Tyler's staying at a friend's house, Hunter won't presume that you did it on purpose. Then, if the dinner turns romantic, you have to let it turn romantic so he sees that you trust him even if he doesn't trust himself. If it doesn't turn romantic, then you simply treat him well and have a good time with him and no one's embarrassed."

"And if he gets romantic without any hint or push from you," Lily added, "then, no matter what he keeps saying, you know there's more behind his gifts than wanting to thank you for raising Tyler or wanting to keep Tyler in his life."

"If he doesn't get romantic," Claire said, picking up where Lily left off. "If he's preoccupied with work, or if he only wants to talk about Tyler, then you'll see you're doing the right thing by pulling back." She took Abby's hand. "You know, you've daydreamed of having Hunter in your life for so long, I'm not surprised you're having trouble getting adjusted to actually having him around. Real love isn't like we thought in high school and you may be looking for

Hunter to say and do things that most men don't say and do."

Abby agreed, but that didn't keep the butterflies out of her stomach when she had to tell Hunter they were eating alone when he arrived in her kitchen that night at six.

"Tyler's staying overnight at Jimmy Parker's," Abby said. Nervous, she dried her hands in her apron to occupy them so she wouldn't fidget.

"Oh," Hunter said, stopping dead in his tracks in front of the door. "What does this mean?"

"It only means that you and I will be eating dinner alone," Abby said, laughing lightly, attempting to downplay the significance of that. "And I made macaroni," she added, then wished she hadn't. Because she was making it sound as if she were *trying* to keep the dinner from getting romantic.

But Hunter wasn't sure what to think. Now that they were accustomed to his work habits and the fact that he would generally come home covered in mud, he stored an extra set of clothes in the laundry room and showered in the downstairs bathroom so he wouldn't track dirt through the bed-and-breakfast. As he made his way down the short hall to the laundry room, retrieved his extra clothes and then stripped in the bathroom, he realized that Abby might be trying so hard to make this look like it wasn't supposed to be a romantic dinner because that was exactly what it was. Or maybe not so much a romantic dinner as an apology evening. After all, she had to realize she had insulted him when she refused the car and she probably felt bad about that—which she should.

Of course, this private evening could have another purpose beyond apology or romance. There were plenty of issues they needed to resolve and it was difficult to discuss them around Tyler because they didn't want to upset him or even concern him. The most logical conclusion to be drawn was that Abby had set up this evening in which they could finalize some issues about Tyler.

So here they were, all by themselves, with time and privacy.

Stepping out of the shower, Hunter decided he didn't know whether to be afraid or curious to see where the evening would lead them. They didn't seem to have a middle of the road. They were either arguing or kissing. It was dangerous for them to be alone.

He recognized he was in for an interesting night, then a mischievous side of himself he thought long buried decided to have a little fun. The woman had refused the gift of a car, the kind of present other people would swoon over. He was literally trying to impress her with his generosity, but she decided it was too much.

He couldn't believe she hadn't recognized that *that* was the point. It was supposed to be an outlandish gift because she had done him an enormous favor. But she wouldn't let him return the favor. Wouldn't let him pay her back or even the score. Almost as if she wanted him to *owe* her.

She had tortured him the entire time he had been home, tempted him with hot responses to his kisses, wouldn't take his back child support so he could feel that he had done his fair share and now seemed to be calling the shots about when and how they talked about Tyler.

Yeah, he definitely felt a little payback was in order. But not the kind he was willing to make on Saturday with the convertible. This time, the payback would be equal to the torment she was dishing out to him.

Wanting to start off small, but very clear about what he planned to do, Hunter simply politely pulled out her chair for her.

"Thank you," she said, her voice wobbling with nerves.

Behind her, Hunter smiled. She'd made him more than nervous all these weeks. She'd made him crazy with lust and kept him terrified that he was going to hurt her. But it suddenly became clear to him that she had done a very good job of protecting herself simply by threatening to kick him out of her home every time she disagreed with him. She could tease him with soft looks and hot kisses one minute and the next minute tug him back in line just by glancing at the door.

Yeah, she deserved an evening of not knowing what to expect.

To throw her off the game, and give her a false sense of security so he could catch her off guard, Hunter said, "I'm assuming you want to get some issues about Tyler straightened out since he's not here."

"That would be a good idea."

"I'm just an idea kind of guy," Hunter agreed, feeling only a tad guilty for the fact that he was about to torment her. In his way of thinking, she needed to see what it felt like to be on the other side of the confusion fence. "What's first on the agenda?"

He asked the question as he took the bowl of macaroni that she offered him. Instead of handling the bowl with care, he deliberately let his hand brush hers. When he reached for the ladle, he tickled his thumb down the side of her little finger.

Then he caught her gaze and smiled at her. "Thank you."

"You're welcome," she said, quickly picking up her fork, Hunter assumed, to make him think she wasn't affected by his touch or the way he looked at her. But in her haste she dropped the utensil and it went clattering to the floor.

"I'll get that," he said and bounced from his seat before she could bend to retrieve it. He took the fork to the sink, then got her another from the silverware drawer.

"Here you go," he said, bending close to her ear as he set her fork beside her plate. As he pulled away, he lightly blew on the back of her neck.

She shivered and shot him a horrified look, but he only smiled innocently. Unless she actually wanted to talk about their sexual attraction, Hunter seriously doubted she would accuse him of anything she couldn't back up with solid proof. He could probably tease her for weeks before she would confront him.

She cleared her throat. "Okay, to kind of get to the point here…"

"Actually, Ab," Hunter said, grabbing her hand as if to snag her attention, but he squeezed her fingers lightly, then held on to her hand as he finished his sentence. "I think we should save the discussion for later. I had a hard day. I'm tired. I would like to eat dinner in peace."

"Okay," she said and the minute her agreement was out of her mouth, he took the fingertips he held loosely in his hand and brought them to his lips.

He kissed them lightly. "Thanks," he said, then kissed them again before he returned her hand to the table.

Abby's toes curled.

There was no way they could talk about the more weighty aspects of their relationship when they were focused on their incredible physical attraction. She didn't know what he was doing, or why he was doing it, but she did know she wasn't saying a word until he stopped this nonsense.

She set her hand on her lap and didn't give him another chance to touch her through dinner, and when it came time for dessert she literally leapt out of her seat so he couldn't beat her to either the coffeepot or the lemon pie.

Feeling proud of herself because she felt she had control again, she didn't even see it coming when Hunter grabbed her hand after taking a bite of pie and groaning in ecstasy. "This is fabulous," he said, pulling her hand to his lips again and kissing each fingertip.

"I didn't make it," she said, her voice trembling. Not only was she confused about what the hell he thought he was proving, but the touch of his smooth, warm lips on her sensitive fingertips was starting to get to her. "Mrs. Romani made it."

Hunter smiled. "Really?" he asked, but his tone questioned why she had gone to extra special trouble.

When she added his thoughts on why she had gone to extra special trouble to all the subtle passes he was making at her, Abby considered that he could actually be physically demonstrating what Kristen had surmised: he had feelings for her that he had trouble expressing except when he was certain Abby was willing to accept them. In creating an environment of security and comfort, Abby had made it possible for him to relax and be himself. In fact, he was behaving so much like the old Hunter that Abby knew that was why she was getting confused. Which could mean Kristen was right, and it would only be a matter of time before Hunter admitted that he loved her.

Or, she suddenly realized looking at his Cheshire cat grin, the new Hunter, the guy with little feelings for anything but Tyler, security and fun, simply could be trying to seduce her because he thought he could. She already knew he believed chivalry was dead, and he could think the quiet, private dinner meant she was willing to be seduced.

"Why don't we finish our dessert in the living room," she suggested, jumping from her chair. Though she knew it would be smarter to follow Kristen's plan, Abby didn't think it wise to play games or even to lure him into security. She had chosen to face this relationship honestly by telling Hunter up front that she wasn't going anywhere, that she trusted him, and that she would step into the relationship he wanted on the condition that he would work toward the relationship she wanted.

Unfortunately, she wasn't ready to do that yet. In the two minutes it would take to get them from the kitchen to the living room, she planned to calm herself.

She also felt a change of scenery would take her mind off the finger kisses and whispery neck warming, until she and Hunter were actually seated, side by side, on the sofa. Then she realized she'd made a tactical error. If he was seducing her, she had just made it easier for him.

"Okay, before we get into something here that neither one of us is really ready to pursue," she said, sliding a few inches away from him on the couch, "I think we ought to talk."

"I don't want to talk about Tyler," Hunter said, scooting closer to her.

She really did want to talk, though not about Tyler, and she didn't want to let Hunter kiss her until he understood her intentions were permanent and serious, not temporary or quasicommitted. But suddenly some of the things Kristen said that afternoon made sense to her. If she continually pulled away from him, or continually acted as though their kissing was somehow wrong, how would he ever get the feeling of security he needed from her? If she wanted him to see that she loved him and he could trust loving her, then she had to quit sliding away from him.

Because she stopped abruptly, he almost bumped into her, but caught himself just in time.

"Now, what were you saying?" he asked, smiling at her with a silly look on his face. He seemed quite proud of the fact that he believed he had trapped her and Abby felt her own female pride rise within her. He wasn't frightening her, pushing her into anything she didn't want to do or even seducing her. If anything, she was inviting him to make the overtures that might be the beginnings of a relationship between them. That being the case, he wasn't getting credit for this moment, for this kiss.

With that thought, she turned suddenly, cupped his cheeks with her hands and pressed her mouth against his.

Hunter hadn't planned to kiss her, but when Abby turned to him with her big green eyes and then made the move that seemed to stun them both, he lost rational thought. Because her arms were raised, he had to settle his hands on her waist to steady himself. When he felt her smallness in his big hands, what brainpower he had left fully deserted him. All he could think about was how wonderful this felt, how right. He knew the purpose of his evening was to give her back exactly what she was giving him, but Abby surprised him by turning the tables again.

Or maybe what she was doing was offering him what he wanted because she finally realized this was what she wanted, too? That more logically explained why she had Tyler out of the house for the entire night.

Buoyed by this knowledge, Hunter got bold and as she kissed him passionately, he allowed his hands to travel up the sides of her waist. When she didn't protest, he slid them a little farther up until they were pressed against the sides of her breasts. When she shivered, but didn't tell him to stop, Hunter figured he had his answers. She had thought this through and she realized he was right, that their commitment to Tyler and their strong physical attraction was enough and she was going to marry him.

With that thought, he lowered them both down on the sofa and took control of the kiss. Hungry but finally feeling in command of his life again, Hunter decided to take everything he wanted right here and right now. Not only because he wanted it, but because he couldn't leave Abby an opening to change her mind. If they were making this decision, they were making it tonight.

But the minute his hand slid beneath the hem of her sweater, Abby felt as though she had been doused with a bucket of cold water. She didn't know how she had managed to get him to take them so far so fast, but she did know she didn't want to go this far without the honest discussion they needed to have. Unfortunately, neither one of them was in the proper frame of mind to have the discussion anymore.

She pushed slightly, causing Hunter to stop his kiss and look at her. Drawing a quick breath, she said, "I don't think I'm ready for this." She used that vague, but accurate, phraseology because she didn't want to insult him and also didn't want to close any doors until they talked.

Looking at his handsome face, she watched him appear to debate. When he slowly shifted away from her, she fumbled to get herself off the sofa quickly and ended up nearly twisted in Hunter's lap. But the feeling of his thighs beneath her bottom seemed to remind her of why it was imperative to leave, and leave now.

She scurried off the sofa and toward the door. She knew she needed to give Hunter at least something of an explanation or he would think she was nuts.

"Actually, Hunter, it isn't only me who isn't ready for this. The truth is, we're not ready as a couple. We need to have a conversation to clear up a few things, but we're also not in the best frame of mind for the discussion tonight." She paused, drew a long breath, then caught his gaze and smiled as best she could. "Good night."

With that, she quickly left the room. Though Hunter knew he could have been annoyed because once again she had yanked the control out of his hands, he felt nothing but happy. She might not be ready for the reality of their commitment, but as far as he was concerned she had made the commitment. And that was what counted.

But he still believed he couldn't let any grass grow under his feet. This decision had been too difficult for her and it was too important to him. He could not give her an opportunity to change her mind.

So the next day he made some special arrangements of his own. First he took the afternoon off work. Since Abby had warned him and Tyler at breakfast that she was working the after-lunch shift for a waitress who had a doctor's appointment, he bought food to cook for supper. When everything was baking, simmering, or waiting to be heated, he ordered flowers for the table and called Mrs. Romani to see if she would take Tyler to the movies then keep him overnight at Grant and Kristen's.

But he made Mrs. Romani promise that she wouldn't let Kristen and Grant know they were keeping Tyler until after the movie. First, he was getting the odd sense that this small-town mentality where everybody knew everybody else's business might be the catalyst of Abby's fear of a less-than-conventional marriage. Second, he just plain didn't want to be interrupted. Abby didn't have to say the words she thought she needed to say. He understood that she was ready to take him as he was, and the kind of relationship he could give her, without expectation of anything further and without regrets. What they needed more than another discussion was the physical commitment. Once they made that commitment, there would be no turning back for either one of them.

And *that,* he realized, was what they both needed.

When Abby arrived home, exhausted and smelling like cooking oil, he directed her upstairs before she had a chance to see the fancy table setting in the dining room or to realize he had every intention of seducing her that night. He told her that since she looked so tired, she should take a bubble bath and relax because his dinner could sit for a while before being eaten.

As he expected, the little bit of pampering went a long way and she came downstairs clean and looking refreshed, and also happy.

But when he led her into the dining room, she froze. "Okay, now I know for sure we need to talk."

"No, we don't," he said from behind her, deliberately tickling her neck with his warm breath as he pulled out her chair and seated her.

"Yes, we do," she contradicted in a firm voice that he had heard her use with Tyler.

He laughed. "Don't waste your time with your intimidating voice. I'm not Tyler. I'm not scared."

His observation made her laugh, but he could still see she was nervous. So he entertained her through dinner with funny stories, and got exactly the result he wanted: she relaxed. It wasn't until they were in the living room, on the same sofa from the night before, that she froze again.

"This isn't right," she said, but Hunter kissed her, and though she tried not to, Abby found herself falling into the kiss. The rational, logical part of her brain reminded her that they needed to talk about a few things before they crossed any lines, but the kiss leapt from passionate to nearly impossible to handle in about thirty seconds and then Abby couldn't think anymore.

She realized that was because the expanded rationale Kristen delivered that afternoon was dancing around in her brain supporting the things she and Hunter were tumbling toward doing. Kristen believed that Hunter kissing Abby was proof positive that they were making progress in getting Hunter comfortable enough to openly, honestly share his love with her. So all of this was right and good.

But suddenly in the midst of the bliss of being kissed by the man she loved, Abby realized that she and Kristen were only guessing about Hunter's feelings. The last rational thought in Abby's brain struggled to the surface again, forcing her to admit that unless or until they talked this out, she really didn't know what he intended.

"Okay," she said, pulling away, "before we get to a place where discussing this would be bad timing, what do you say we discuss it now?"

"We don't need to discuss anything," Hunter said, then pulled her up for a long, openmouthed kiss.

Refusing to be deterred, she yanked herself away the very second an opportunity presented itself. "I'm serious. You want to be with Tyler as much as possible, you want to be as much of a father as possible to him and you think marrying me will accomplish that."

Hunter began kissing her neck. "I *know* marrying you will accomplish that."

Shivering with need, Abby drew a long breath. "And I agree. So we have some points of agreement, but we still have one really big point of disagreement."

In between little nipping bites on her earlobe, Hunter said, "I can't imagine what that would be."

His answer was enough to take her attention off the bites to her ear. "Our problem is the same one we've always had," she said, incredulous that he could have forgotten. "You want to create a family. I want love."

"If we make a family, you'll get lots of love."

His statement started a bubble of hope to form in

her chest but she knew she needed to push his admissions the whole way before she could make love with him.

She forced him to look at her. Serious, desperately hopeful, she said, "Will I? Will I get lots of love?"

"Of course, you will," he said simply and would have kissed her again, but Abby stopped him.

"Love of the wonderful, passionate kind I want from you?"

To Hunter's credit, he didn't lie to her. "Abby, you know I believe the kind of love you want doesn't exist."

"And you know that I disagree. I not only think it exists, I can't make a commitment to you unless I have your promise that you will at least *try* to love me. All I'm asking you to do, Hunter, is say that you'll try to love me. Really love me. Like you used to."

She could tell by the tortured look in his eyes that he knew exactly what she was talking about, that he remembered the deep passionate intimate love they shared, but he didn't want it. And by being able to resist it he felt himself stronger or more of a man. So he wouldn't lie to her by saying he would try, because strong decisive men didn't hedge the truth either. He didn't need to. This empty shell of a relationship that seemed to consist primarily of sex and parenting was enough for him.

"What about me?" she asked, finishing her thought out loud, then swallowing the lump in her throat. "Am I supposed to do without that love, too?"

"Abby, your idea of love is highly idealized."

She lifted her chin. "I don't think so."

"I do," he said.

For what seemed like an eternity, he only stared at

her, then he shook his head as if amazed that she couldn't see he was right, and rose from the sofa.

"Don't bother telling me that I have to leave the bed-and-breakfast," he said, sounding more annoyed than hurt by their inability to work things out. "This time it's my choice."

Chapter Eleven

Abby wasn't surprised when the Brewster women arrived at the diner ten minutes after her shift began. Not really wanting to avoid them, but not ready to discuss her painful conversation with Hunter from the night before, Abby was grateful for the abundance of customers who kept her busy. Finally, when the diner began to clear, she took a seat in the booth with the three women and their rambunctious triplets.

"It's over," she said as calmly as she could, given that she was heartbroken. "I don't want to talk about it. I don't want to hear any more good ideas or plan any new strategies. I'm done. Not because I don't recognize that in his own way he loves me, but because I finally see he doesn't *want* to be intimate with me. I'm done kidding myself, I'm done testing and I'm done experimenting."

Something in her voice must have touched the Brewster wives because each cast a quick glance at the others, before Claire finally said, "You know what? We're sorry."

Abby waved her dishcloth in dismissal. "You don't have anything to be sorry for."

"We pushed you," Kristen softly admitted.

"Somebody had to push me," Abby said, then rose from the booth. "But I think it was for the best. I needed to know with absolute certainty that giving up was the right thing to do. Now I know it is."

Surprisingly, it was Lily who didn't seem as convinced as the others. "Are you sure?"

"I finally realized that if I stayed in that relationship, I wouldn't only be shortchanging myself, I would also be shortchanging Hunter. You see, the thing is," she admitted quietly, "his eyes tell me he knows exactly what he's missing by not having an intimate, trusting relationship. There's just too much history between us for him to reach out for it again."

"And you think that there might be another woman out there who could make him regain his ability to trust?" Kristen speculated quietly.

She nodded.

"Boy, you're braver than I am," Claire said, placing her hand atop Abby's where it rested on the table of the booth.

"Stronger than I am," Lily said, laying her hand on Claire's.

"Certainly less selfish than I am," Kristen said, putting her hand on top of Lily's.

"But we support you," Claire said.

Abby drew a long breath for courage, then swallowed the lump in her throat. She might not have Hunter Wyman's love, but she had the love of some very, very good friends. "Thank you," she said, con-

fident that she had made the right decision no matter
how much it hurt.

When Hunter came into the diner with Grant for
lunch that afternoon, Abby began to tremble. If she
thought learning to live without him had been difficult
when he was away, she now realized that trying to
live without him when he could show up almost anywhere in her world would be close to impossible.

But Abby had survived the deaths of both of her
parents, assumed financial and business responsibilities that were over her head and raised a child alone
for several years. She refused to let this ruin her.

However, she wasn't going to be so foolish as to
wait on him the day after he chose to leave her home.
She directed Sally Whiteford, the diner's other lunch
waitress to get the table, and, oblivious, Sally com-
plied. Then she went into the pantry behind the kitchen
and leaned across the butcher-block table, taking deep
breaths to get her bearings. She needed a minute to
recharge her reserves.

"Hey, what the heck are you doing in here?"

Abby's head jerked up and she saw big, stormy
Grant Brewster standing in the doorway of the pantry.

"Actually, Grant, I'm breathing."

Where that answer might have confused another
person, or at least caused him to question Abby, it
seemed to make perfect sense to Grant, who strolled
a little farther into the room. "You okay?"

"I will be in another thirty seconds or so. Then I
have tons of work to do," she reminded him pointedly,
hoping he would take the hint.

"You know, Hunter is every bit as miserable as you
are."

"I'm not miserable," Abby quickly retorted. "I just needed some air."

"Well, even if you're not miserable, Hunter is."

"That's not my problem," Abby said, shifting away from the butcher-block table and straightening her apron, preparing to leave the pantry.

"The heck it isn't!" Grant said through a groan. "Come on, Abby. I'm not stupid and I'm not blind. I know the two of you have been trying to put a relationship together, if only because you have a son."

Abby blew her breath out on a sigh. "If you've figured all that out, then you should also have realized that it didn't work."

Grant groaned again. "You hardly tried!"

"The hell I didn't," Abby said, getting angry now. "I tried everything. Being nice, being understanding, making the first move, giving him privileges with Tyler, letting him live with us, accepting gifts he bought for Tyler to give me. I tried and tried." She cast him a curious, but still angry look. "Don't you talk to your wife?"

"Yeah, but she's pretty closemouthed when it comes to you because she says this is one of those women confidences that men can't understand."

Picturing petite, sugar-sweet Kristen standing up to her huge, fearless husband made Abby smile. "She's exactly right."

"No, you're all wrong. And it's stupid to have a relationship by consensus anyway. You and Hunter have to decide for yourselves, Abby."

"Grant, we did," Abby said. "We always knew we wanted two completely different things. Last night we just realized neither one of us planned to change our minds."

"Couldn't you compromise?" he pleaded.

"Why?" she asked incredulously. "What's it to you?"

"My sanity," Grant said. "Hunter is miserable and he's driving *me* nuts!"

Finally recognizing what was going on, Abby pushed past Grant, shaking her head. "You're impossible. I'm not going to have a relationship with Hunter just to make sure your project stays on target."

"The more miserable he is, the more chance we'll make a mistake," Grant said, following her through the kitchen. "Come on, Abby, the whole county is depending upon this project. You can't let us down."

His argument about the community didn't faze her one bit. But when she reached the door that led to the dining room and saw Hunter sitting in one of the booths against the wall of windows on the far side of the building, she stopped dead in her tracks. The one thing she hadn't counted on in her quest to get over Hunter was that seeing him miserable would be so hard on her. Her own wretchedness was difficult enough to handle, but it was nearly impossible to see him suffer without feeling that she had to do something to rectify it.

Squeezing her eyes shut, she wondered if by all her pushing and experimenting she hadn't moved them out of the relationship too soon, as Grant indicated.

"That's right, look at him," Grant said from behind her. "He's sad. He's lonely."

Seeing his slumped shoulders and the faraway look on his face as he stared out the window at Brewster's sparse traffic, Abby felt herself weakening.

"He loves that boy," Grant whispered in Abby's ear. "And you're taking Tyler away from him."

Abby felt like a balloon that had suddenly lost its air.

She faced Grant. "What?"

"He loves Tyler," Grant said insistently. "Don't take him away."

Anger put color in her cheeks. So, Hunter had lied about what had happened between them. "I didn't take Tyler away. Hunter himself chose to leave. And he can visit Tyler any time he wants," she coolly informed. "*And* he knows this," she added, giving her apron waistband a quick, determined yank, then walking away from Grant Brewster.

She couldn't believe she had been so blind and so stupid. Hunter only wanted Tyler in his life, not her. The proof was in what Hunter had told his best friend and partner, Grant Brewster. He missed Tyler. He didn't want to be away from Tyler. He didn't say one word about her. Though she was hurt and mad, Abby took a minute to be grateful that Hunter cared for Tyler, loved him, wanted to be part of his life, because her son needed that from him.

Then she let the anger consume her because she wasn't going to be weak or foolish again. Hunter wanted to be Tyler's full-time dad and to do that he felt he had to marry her. That was the extent of what he felt for her. She had to remember that.

It was after seven when Hunter arrived at the bed-and-breakfast to retrieve his belongings. Abby realized he had not only found somewhere to clean up after work, but also, he was late enough that she and Tyler had already eaten. She suspected that was because he had come to the same conclusions she had. A marriage between them wouldn't work and they had to pull away from each other. He needed to focus his attention solely on Tyler. And she needed to allow him to do that.

But she also decided that she couldn't stay angry with him or ignore him because that wouldn't do anybody any good. So, when he knocked on the door and she granted him entry, she smiled at him. "Look, I'm really sorry for the argument last night."

He glanced around as if having trouble with his feelings over remembering the argument, confirming for her that he had trouble dealing with feelings in general. He kept his life neat and clean and predictable so he wouldn't have any overwhelming or intense emotions and in a good many ways, Abby supposed she didn't blame him. Most of his life had not been pleasant.

Her wanting a passionate relationship from him was almost cruel. She was asking him to take down the barriers that protected him from the hurts of the past and he couldn't do that. In that second, with that realization, Abby felt the door of destiny closing. He had made himself this way for a reason. His decision had been permanent. She had the choice of accepting him the way he was or moving on.

Tyler came bounding into the room. "Hunter!" he said, screeching to a halt. "You missed supper."

Hunter stooped to his son's level. "I ate with Grant and Kristen. And," he said, drawing the word out as if giving himself time to carefully choose how he would phrase his next revelation, "I'm going to be staying with Grant and Kristen from now on."

Tyler's mouth fell and he blinked rapidly. "What?"

"From now on I'm going to be staying with Kristen

and Grant. Grant and I have a lot of work to do. This way we can get it all done.''

"Oh," Tyler said, disappointment dripping through the one syllable.

"So, why don't you come upstairs and help me gather my things?''

"Okay," Tyler agreed slowly.

Abby was flooded by guilt. When Hunter rose and put his hands on Tyler's shoulder, the degree of the guilt intensified because the look on Hunter's face was every bit as forlorn as the look on her son's.

And she couldn't shake the notion that it was her fault. She also couldn't excuse it. All she had to do was ask Hunter to forget about what happened the night before and come back to the bed-and-breakfast, and Tyler and Hunter would be happy again.

Surely she could handle that. She would bump into the man a hundred times a week anyway. By keeping him out of her home she wasn't giving herself a reprieve from seeing him. Brewster was much too small of a town.

Unhappy and confused, Abby sneaked up the back stairway, fully intending to tell Hunter they should give his living at the bed-and-breakfast one more try. She actually contemplated telling him to have his lawyer draw up some kind of official documentation that would set boundaries and limits for both of them that would assure that they would stick to whatever deal they made.

But when she reached his room and heard the interplay between father and son she stopped dead in her tracks, simply enjoying the moment. She listened to the laughter. She listened to Hunter's quiet words of assurance to Tyler that everything would be okay.

She listened as Tyler asked about the lizards in the wetland. She listened as Hunter gave a response through semi-muffled chuckles.

Her eyes filled with tears. This was why she couldn't have Hunter live in her house. Not because she didn't want him and Tyler sharing these intimate father and son moments, but because these moments should be family moments, but she wasn't invited. She really wasn't a part of their relationship. She was someone separate. And it would hurt every time one of these moments occurred and she was forced to back away and let them enjoy their love for each other.

She finally saw the thing that had been bothering her since Hunter returned. He had no trouble being passionately in love with his son. He had no trouble putting his emotional well-being on the line with his little boy. He could be vulnerable. He *was* vulnerable. He didn't seem to mind aching with grief over losing time with his son.

Which meant it was possible for him to love without thought for the consequences. He simply couldn't do it for her.

With a hand over her mouth to stifle her sobs, she turned away from the bedroom and let her son and his father have their privacy. Because this was the rest of her life and it was time for her to get used to it. Hunter would soon get a home that Tyler would make a second home and she wouldn't be invited.

In the kitchen, she calmed herself by searching her cookbook for a quick, easy cookie recipe, but realized baking cookies wouldn't do her any good. She wanted to pound something and decided the only thing that required pounding was bread dough. She leafed through the book again and found the right recipe and immediately gathered the ingredients. By the time Hunter and Tyler came into her kitchen, she was up to her elbows in flour and most of her frustrations had been pounded into the dough.

"All set?" she asked, feigning cheerfulness as she turned from the counter to face them.

"All set," Hunter said grimly.

It wasn't the tone of his voice or even his pain that got to her. Even Tyler's pain didn't penetrate the logic she clung to to remind her of why they couldn't live together. It was the way Hunter nestled Tyler's little hand into his larger one. In the entire time Hunter had lived with them, she rarely saw him touch their son in a gesture of affection. He put his hand on Tyler's shoulder to stop him or hold him where he was. He tickled him. He tossed him. He roughhoused with the best of them. But he rarely took Tyler's hand. When he did, it meant something.

Feeling like the Wicked Witch of the West, Abby cleared her throat. "I could help you carry your stuff out to your car," she volunteered quietly.

"No, thank you," Hunter said. Then he hunkered down beside his son. "I'll be here on Saturday," he said comfortingly. Again, Abby felt a stab of guilt that almost changed her mind. "You be ready at nine and we'll spend the entire day together." He glanced up at Abby. "Including dinner, if that's okay with you."

"Sure," Abby said, her throat closing again.

"Now, you run along," he said to Tyler. "Your mother and I still have a few things to discuss."

Tyler nodded and the dejected look on his face did Abby in. She had never in her life deliberately deprived her son of anything, particularly not because

she placed her needs above his, and she couldn't believe she was starting now.

"Hunter," she began after Tyler sadly left the room,
"I—"

"No," Hunter said, stopping her. "Before you say
anything, I want the chance to have my say. I won't
tolerate Tyler doing without anything, not *anything*,"
he said, "because you're too stubborn or too proud to
take my money." He fished into his wallet and pulled
out five hundred dollars, which he slammed on the
kitchen table. "And maybe if you would buy something for yourself once in a while, treat yourself good
every once in a while, you wouldn't—"

"Be so unreasonable?" Abby said, swallowing the
lump of hurt that formed in her throat. "I have every
intention of taking child support," she said, her chin
lifting. "But I want to get two things straight with you.
First, I did all right by Tyler without your money. He
never did without. Second, I'm not unreasonable."

Hunter ran his hand along the back of his neck.
"Look, I'm sorry. That was a cheap shot."

"It's okay," Abby said, "I understand."

"Do you?" Hunter asked suddenly, catching her
gaze and holding it. "Do you understand what it's like
to know you have a son, that you missed the first six
years of his life and now you're only going to get bits
and pieces?"

Abby simply stared at him, her eyes filling with
tears. "Frankly, Hunter, I think I have a much clearer
understanding of what you feel about not quite being
a part of things than you think I do. I think it's my
side of things that you don't understand."

Hunter laughed bitterly. "Boy, you know, I heard

conversations like this one in divorce court every day I was there.''

''Then I guess we can thank goodness we didn't get married.''

''I guess we can,'' he agreed with a nod before he headed for the door. But he stopped suddenly. ''For the record, I wish I believed in everything you want. I really do. But I don't see it. I don't see it happening for us.''

With that he walked out the door and Abby fell to a seat by her kitchen table. If he hadn't said ''for us'' Abby might not have felt empty and wounded. She sincerely doubted he realized what he had said, but it was the thing that had nagged Abby all along.

He didn't trust her.

And he would eventually trust someone else. Not only was he going to take half of Tyler's love, but also someday, maybe even soon, she would have to handle watching him fall in love with another woman.

Chapter Twelve

When Abby awakened the next morning, she thought the sun was particularly bright. Then she wondered why she hadn't heard her alarm. She hadn't fallen asleep until after midnight, alternating between worrying that she had done the wrong thing with Hunter and crying because she finally accepted she would never have his love. She couldn't believe she would have awakened before her seven o'clock alarm.

When she looked at the clock and saw it was nine-thirty, her mouth dropped open in dismay. She *knew* she had set her alarm. Yet, the button was in the Off position.

She bounced out of bed and bounded into Tyler's room, only to discover he was not only up, he had made his bed. That shocked her so much she almost didn't notice the note he had pinned to his pillow.

Thinking it was a six-year-old version of an apology for being sullen the night before, Abby picked it up with a smile. But when she saw he hadn't drawn the customary picture on the sheet, she quickened her fingers. When she read his simple first grade explanation that he was going to look for Hunter, Abby threw the paper on the bed and virtually flew down the stairs.

She grabbed the phone and quickly punched in the number for Grant and Kristen's house. "Is Hunter there?" she asked Mrs. Romani when the older woman picked up the phone.

"Why, yes, honey, he's right here," she said happily.

Abby squeezed her eyes shut in relief, thinking Tyler must already be at the Brewster house for Mrs. Romani to be so cheerful.

But when Hunter said, "Hello, Abby," very quietly, all her relief fled.

She swallowed hard. "Hunter, I found a note on Tyler's bed this morning. He's on his way to find you."

"What?" Hunter asked with a gasp.

"I'm sorry," she said. "I got to bed late. I thought I set my alarm, but it was off. I just woke up now, ran into his room and found the note."

"Oh, damn it!" Hunter said, sounding frustrated. "Abby, last night when we were packing my things, I explained to Tyler where Grant's house was. Damn it," he said, obviously remembering something else. "I also explained how to turn off an alarm clock when he asked about it. He asks so many odd questions sometimes, I didn't think anything of his asking about the alarm clock last night and never made the connection about Grant's house. Damn it!"

"Well, let's not panic," Abby said calmly, feeling her first kinship with her child's father in a long, long time. "He's on his way to find you. So, he's on Route

160. Not the best place for a six-year-old boy on a bike, but at least we know we can find him.''

"You're right. And I'm sorry, Abby,'' Hunter said. "I should have asked him why he wanted to know where Grant lives. Even worse, I should have asked why he wanted to know how to turn off an alarm.''

"You're new at being a father,'' Abby said, accepting his apology. "Don't be too hard on yourself.''

"Right,'' Hunter said. "I'll go drive 160 now and get him.''

"Good. Bring him to the diner, please?''

"Okay,'' Hunter agreed congenially.

Though worried about her son, Abby finally felt some peace about her relationship with Hunter. She would never have his love. She would never be his wife. But they could be Tyler's parents. Deep down inside, both of them were mature adults.

She called the diner to explain why she'd be late, then quickly dressed in her waitress uniform and went to work. She had to go about her day as necessary until Hunter brought her son to her. Then she wasn't sure how she would discipline him, if she would discipline him or even what she would say. But she did know she had to teach him that he couldn't alternate between her house and Hunter's current residence without first getting permission.

When ten o'clock became eleven and there was still no sign of Hunter or Tyler, Abby felt herself grow frantic. Ten minutes later Hunter arrived at the diner alone. He took her to a booth and sat her down before he said, "Abby, I obviously didn't find him.''

Abby forced a laugh. "Here, I thought you were keeping him in your SUV so you and I could have another one of our famous disastrous discussions.''

"I wish," Hunter said softly. "Grant called the state police. Kristen is rounding up a search party. I have to go, too, but we'll keep you informed."

"The hell you will," Abby said, bouncing from her seat. Fear poured through her, and so did guilt. She was the one who caused Tyler to go in search of his father. "I can't sit here and wait for you! I *won't* sit here and wait for you!"

"You also can't go out like this," Hunter said calmly. "Abby, this is a hard thing to do."

She drew a long breath and pierced him with a level look. "I can handle it."

"I'm sure you can. But for now, we need you here to talk with the state police when they arrive. We also need to know where you are so we can tell you immediately when one of us finds him."

Because that made sense, Abby sank to the bench seat of the booth again. "Okay."

Hunter squeezed her hands. "You wait here for the state police. Kristen's on her way. So are Lily and Claire."

As if saying her name had some kind of magic, Claire burst through the door of the diner. "Abby, honey, don't worry," she said soothingly. "Evan has sent every employee of the lumber mill out to the woods. They should find him really quickly."

"Good," Abby said, feeling numb. She didn't even notice that Hunter kissed her forehead before he walked out the diner door to go in search of their son.

With Claire and Lily at her side, she spoke with the state police. Then she sat in the booth and waited. The only patrons who came into the diner were searchers in need of a break. Hunter never came in, indicating to Abby that something was wrong. When he finally did arrive at the diner a little past two, Abby refused to let him leave her behind again.

"This is my son," she said urgently, gripping the collar of Hunter's plaid shirt in her straining fingers. "I know him better than anyone. I can find him."

"Abby, experienced hunters and woodsmen are in that forest and none of us has even turned up a clue."

"Has anyone talked to Jimmy Parker?" Abby asked. "He might know of a cabin they built or a cave they found."

"Yes, Abby," Hunter said. "The state trooper talked with Jimmy Parker. We've exhausted all his leads."

"Where is he?" Abby said, then balled her fists in anger. "Damn it. Where is he?"

"We'll find him, Abby," Hunter assured her.

But Abby shook her head. "*I'll* find him," she said, storming out of the diner.

"At least change your clothes," Hunter said, scurrying after her.

"No," she shot back, bounding toward her house where she would get her old car and drive to the section of forest that separated Brewster mansion from town. "There are no more sturdy, more comfortable shoes than these," she said, indicating her utilitarian waitress footwear. "I'm not leaving him alone in the woods one more second."

"Okay," he said, grabbing her arm to stop her. "You can go. You can go in your uniform. But you can't take that car. Come with me in the SUV."

They drove to the stretch of woods where Tyler was most likely to be found. Each side of the two-lane road was lined with the vehicles of the searchers. Hunter explained that they had started out combing the first four feet into the woods for the entire length of the distance between the beginning of the forest and Grant's house. When they completed that section, each team had been instructed to move in another four feet.

Getting out of the car, Abby glanced around, then caught Hunter's attention. "Did you specifically tell him to take this road to get to Grant's house?"

Hunter shook his head. "No, but because it's the only road to Grant's house from town, I assumed he knew to take it."

"He could have simply gone through the woods," Abby said, observing the scene around her. "Before he died, my father would take Tyler for short walks into the woods behind the bed-and-breakfast. Once we had a picnic by a small stream and my father explained that old Mr. Brewster's house was just beyond that stream."

Hunter looked mortified. "I told him Grant's house was at the end of the woods. I assumed he would travel by road. I never thought he would take the entire forest route."

"Let's go," Abby said, directing Hunter back into his SUV. "We'll let these guys continue the logical search, but just in case Tyler remembered what my father told him, we'll start searching the woods behind the bed-and-breakfast."

They made the trip back through town and to Abby's house quickly. Hunter even knew an old logging road that took them almost halfway into the forest. With no more than a dirt path in front of them, they got out of the sport utility vehicle and began to walk.

Abby led Hunter to the stream where she, her father

and Tyler had had their picnic, and suddenly, unexpectedly, she began to laugh.

"What's funny?" Hunter asked quietly, knowing it was tension that had her laughing, but needing to get them both talking if only to calm their frazzled nerves.

"When he was little, Tyler couldn't say orange. He would say O-Ringe." She shook her head. "I don't know why I thought of that now."

"Because it's cute. It's a cute memory," Hunter said, his eyes filling with tears. He'd found his son after six years and now, because of his inability to get along with his son's mother, he might have lost him. "What else do you remember?" he whispered as he put his arm around Abby's shoulders and pulled her close to him.

She sniffed and wiped a tear off her cheek. "He slept with a ratty old blanket until about three days before you arrived. One night he suddenly brought it into my room and told me he didn't need it and I could throw it away."

"Thank God," Hunter said, feeling the need to tease her. "I wouldn't want any son of mine to sleep with a blanket."

"He's only six," Abby said plaintively. "If he wanted a blanket, he should have been allowed to have a blanket." She paused, swallowed hard. "But that night he told me he was a big boy and didn't need a blanket anymore." She sniffed again. "It used to make me feel guilty that he thought he should be protecting me."

"He loves you," Hunter said, wishing with all his heart that he could love her, too. He had so many feelings for her. Gratitude. Appreciation. Respect. Admiration. Desire. Everything but unconditional love.

Because he thought unconditional love was for fools and he wouldn't set himself up to be a fool again. "You made him into a little man, Abby, without even having any help or guidance. That says a lot," he said, and squeezed her shoulders.

They made it to the creek and Abby immediately spotted the little footprints in the soft earth by the shore. "He was here," she said quietly, but fear put a quiver in her voice. In a woods filled with wild animals and dangerous terrain, it wasn't safe for a little boy to be alone.

"We'll find him," Hunter said, moving in front of her and putting his hands on her shoulders. Because he had never looked back when he left Brewster County, he had forced those shoulders to bear a lot of responsibility and a lot of pain and for that he was deeply sorry. "I promise we'll find him."

She nodded and they walked along the narrow stream until they found a shallow point at which they could cross. The forest began to thicken and the underbrush became more dense and harder to navigate. A few minutes later they found Tyler's abandoned bike and Abby choked back tears.

Pressing his lips together to hide their trembling, Hunter held her while she cried. "We'll find him," he said, the phrase becoming something of a litany. When her weeping subsided, he said, "But I think right now, we need to tell the others what we've found. Let's walk back to the SUV and use my car phone."

She shook her head fiercely. "We're this close and the sun will be setting in a few hours. We can't waste time."

Because he agreed with her Hunter allowed her to lead him farther into the woods. They reached a point where her knowledge of the forest decreased, but his increased. "My father's farm was just over there," he said, pointing to the west to orient her. "When I was little I would come out here to get away from him if he had been drinking. In fact," he said, glancing around, "there's a cave over there."

"A cave!" Abby cried, horrified. "Bears live in caves."

"Don't panic," Hunter said, grabbing her hand to lead her in the right direction. He didn't tell her about the cliff to the right of the cave, or the field of brier bushes to the left. At this point, the cave was looking like the best alternative.

They pushed on for another twenty minutes and Hunter realized Abby was getting exhausted. He tricked her into stopping for a few minutes, and just as they were about to rise and begin their walk again, they heard Tyler's voice.

"Mom! Mom!" he cried, the small voice getting closer, the sound of moving shrubbery coming from the left.

"Tyler!" Hunter called. He pivoted to the left, then looked up and down until he spotted his son. "Tyler!" he said, and without thought for Abby, ran toward him.

"Dad!" Tyler ran into Hunter's arms and allowed himself to be scooped off the ground. His cheeks were tearstained. His grubby T-shirt was torn. "Oh, Dad! It's scary out here. There are bugs! A bee almost bit me!"

"I know. I know," Hunter said, laughing through his tears. Hot passionate love poured through him. For the first time, his son had called him dad and the mere sound of the word seemed to resonate through his entire being. Tyler loved him enough to accept him unconditionally. He hadn't known how much he wanted it, hadn't known how desperately he needed it, until Tyler called him dad.

Then he looked over and saw Abby. Standing off to the right, relieved and chomping at the bit to get to her son, she nonetheless let Hunter have his moment. The most generous person Hunter had ever met, she wouldn't interfere in his relationship with his son, but in hanging back she missed out on the moment. She missed all this wonderful love. She was alone, waiting.

And in that second he understood that he hadn't merely blocked her from receiving his love, he was edging her out of special, wonderful moments with their son.

The knowledge that he could be so wrong almost paralyzed him. He slid Tyler to the ground. The little boy instantly ran to his mother.

"Mom! I was so scared."

"I know," she said, catching him when he catapulted himself at her. Peppering his face with kisses, she said, "You're a big boy, but you still need somebody to help you in the woods."

"I know!" Tyler emphatically agreed through little choking sobs.

And Hunter knew they wouldn't punish him. Tyler had learned a valuable lesson and was scared enough that he would never pull a stunt like this again. Of course, Hunter would privately explain to Tyler that he should never again turn off his mother's alarm and neither should he set out on any adventures without first asking permission. But for now, he would let Abby have her moment of relief. He would let her spoil their son.

In the SUV, Hunter called the state police and Grant and let them know Tyler had been found. The search was called off. Hunter, Tyler and Abby met with the trooper one final time, and then everyone went home.

As soon as they entered the bed-and-breakfast, Abby put a roast in the oven as if it were any other day. Hunter took Tyler to his room to help him change out of his soiled clothes. Though Abby checked on them, she didn't involve herself too much further. Instead, she announced that she also needed to get out of her waitress uniform and into regular clothes.

Hunter felt another stab of guilt, and an overwhelming sadness. He thought at first that he was pushing her out of her son's life and that was the cause of this pain, then he realized that wasn't true.

He felt the sadness because he was hurting someone he loved.

He loved her.

Desperately.

Passionately.

And all he ever did was hurt her.

Chapter Thirteen

"Abby, I love you."

Abby didn't even look up from the potatoes she was preparing. "I love you, too, Hunter," she said, stirring briskly as she read the directions on the side panel of a box.

"No," he said, walking over to her. He took the empty container from her hands and set it on the counter top. "I really love you."

"Uh-huh," she said, then picked up her box with the directions again and went back to reading.

"Damn it, Abby!" he said, spinning her to face him. "I said I love you."

"All right, stop it," Abby said, slamming the package on the counter top. "I've already decided I'm not going to kick you out of the bed-and-breakfast again. You and I will raise Tyler together. In fact, I'll go see Chas Brewster and ask him to draw up some kind of an agreement that gives you the security you need to have with Tyler. So, you can stop now."

"I don't want to stop now," he said, wonderful joy flowing through him. He loved her. He loved her the way he used to love her. Memories came flooding back, but more than that, a sense of the rightness in the present and the beauty of the future were a panoramic vision before him. *"I love you."*

"Yeah, right," Abby said, shrugging away from him. "Look, Hunter, I'm not a psychiatrist, but you've had a scare with your son. It's making you a little crazy. So stop before you say something you're going to regret."

"I'm not going to regret this," he assured her, again grabbing her shoulders and pulling her against him. "I love you."

Abby sagged in his arms. "You love me in this moment because you're relieved," she explained again, as if tired of having to repeat herself. "And you also love me because I'm your son's mother. But I need more than that."

"I know and I'm ready to give it."

"Yeah, right," she said, pushing out of his hold. "Call Tyler for dinner."

Hurt and amazed, he stared at her. "Why won't you believe me?"

"Because we've been down this road before. The only thing that has changed is that this is the first time you've actually dangled the only real bait that would entice me. Look, you're getting what you want. You will live with Tyler. But I've found a nice safe place for my heart and I don't want you disrupting things by saying you love me. Just back off and let me alone, okay?"

He would have argued, except he saw the tears that pooled in her eyes and he knew he had hurt her once too often. But more than that, he suddenly saw what was going on: she'd turned the tables. He'd played the role of a man guarding his heart so well, he'd taught her how to do it for herself.

"What did you expect?" Grant Brewster asked, when Hunter admitted what had happened the night before. "Here's a woman who has your son, raises him alone and literally waits seven years for you to come home to straighten out your problems, and the way you thank her is to tell her you can't love her."

Hunter heard everything Grant had said, but he got stuck on the waiting seven years part. "She waited for me?"

"Never dated a soul…except Evan, but that didn't count because everybody knew Evan was only asking her out to avoid Claire."

Though the story sounded like a good one, Hunter decided to forgo hearing it until he understood the facts about Abby. "She never dated anyone?"

"Nope. She said she was busy with her sick parents and raising Tyler, but the girls told me they always knew she was waiting for you."

"And why didn't anybody tell *me?*"

"Most of us thought it was fairly obvious from her behavior," Kristen put in from the den door. "Hunter, really, the woman tried and tried. I gave her at least two ideas to try to reach you. I know Claire's been counseling her as well. And Lily thinks you're just plain thickheaded."

"Well, thank you all for that vote of confidence."

"What do you want?" Kristen asked incredulously. "You broke that woman's heart so many times and you think you can do it with impunity, or that she won't be afraid of you, or that she won't wise up and protect herself?''

"I already figured a lot of that out myself."

"So what do you want?"

"I don't know. Advice?"

"The only advice that's going to mean anything has to come from right here," Kristen said, storming into the room and poking her index finger at his chest. "If a really good idea doesn't come from your heart, you don't deserve her."

"I sort of agree, Hunter," Grant said, but at least he had the decency to squirm in his seat. "Abby's one of the nicest, sweetest people in the world and you treated her badly. If you can't figure out how to win her back yourself, then maybe you don't deserve her."

Sufficiently put in his place, Hunter rose. If it wouldn't have been for the fact that he understood what Grant and Kristen were telling him, Hunter might have been angry with the advice. Because he did understand, because he finally saw how much he had hurt Abby, because he actually believed he deserved punishment—no matter how much he didn't like it—he drew a long breath and headed out the door.

He was supposed to return to the bed-and-breakfast. He was living there now officially, because Abby was generous. But he felt really odd about going back. Unless or until he could convince her to marry him, he would be putting her in the position of being on the outside of the circle he was creating with Tyler.

And he refused to hurt her anymore.

Refused!

Now, if he could just figure out how the hell to get her to realize he truly did love her, passionately, desperately and forever.

* * *

Abby was awakened by the sound of pebbles hitting her window. At first she almost panicked, thinking Jimmy Parker was trying to get Tyler out of bed and outside in the middle of the night, then she smiled to herself thinking the kid wasn't about to awaken Tyler since he was hitting the wrong window. Let him toss pebbles to his heart's delight. Eventually he would give up.

But the little dickens was persistent.

And annoying.

After ten minutes of it Abby tossed off her covers and stormed to the window. She yanked it open and was just about to give Jimmy a piece of her mind when she saw Hunter sitting on a white horse in her backyard and her mouth dropped open.

"Hey, Abby," he said, grinning.

"What are you doing?" she asked incredulously.

"I'm here to rescue my princess from her dull, boring life."

"Go to bed, Hunter," she said and was closing her window when he waved a roll of aluminum foil at her.

"Don't make me use this," he said. "If I have to I'll wrap myself up in this aluminum foil so that I really look like your knight in shining armor, but I don't want to have to go that far." He glanced around. "I think the neighbors are going to talk enough about the fact that I rode a white horse down Main Street in the middle of the night. I don't want to give them more fodder for the gristmill."

She stopped her efforts to close her window, but she didn't say anything, only stared at Hunter in amazement.

"Look, Abby," he said, sounding contrite and sad,

"I made a lot of mistakes. A lot. The biggest being that I didn't relax. I brought too much baggage home with me and though that's not an excuse for treating you badly, it's at least a reason. Or an explanation. But I don't think it's a big enough mistake to banish me from the kingdom forever."

"I'm listening," Abby said, leaning forward on the window.

"Okay." He drew a long breath. "I love you and I want to marry you." He raked his fingers through his hair in frustration. "Hell, I'll even marry you on the white horse if it'll sway your decision. But I want to marry you. Not for Tyler. And not even to assure that I can be the kind of father for Tyler that I can only be if I live with you. I want to marry you for you. To love you." He stopped and looked down at his hands, which were clutching the grazing horse's reins. "Just to love you," he said slowly, and with more emotion than Abby had heard from him since he had found Tyler in the woods.

Blinking back tears, she closed her bedroom window then raced down the stairs and out her back door. When she reached the porch, she saw Hunter had dismounted and tied the horse to the porch rail. She rushed into his open arms and he kissed her.

When she finally pulled away, Abby smiled at him. "You know I didn't need the horse to believe you. I only needed to hear in your voice that you really loved me."

"I love you," he emphatically assured her. "You're the only person for whom I would ever do something this foolish." Then without a word of warning, he scooped her up and set her on the horse and hoisted himself to the saddle behind her.

"What are you doing?" Abby said with a giggle.

"Shhh. Nothing," Hunter whispered. "Hey, Mrs. McClosky," he called and Abby saw the gossipy elementary school principal was staring out her dining room window at them.

"How about coming over and watching Tyler for about an hour? The back door's open," Hunter yelled. "You can have this roll of aluminum foil for your trouble."

The old woman ran to her back porch and looked as though she would argue, but before she could say a word, Hunter tossed the roll of foil at her. "For your trouble," he said and turned the horse toward the woods.

"What if she doesn't do it?" Abby giggled.

"Oh, she won't let Tyler stay alone," Hunter said chuckling. "Besides, think of the story she's going to have to tell tomorrow."

Abby couldn't have agreed more. They were riding off into the woods, summer moonlight glistening off the perfect white horse. Abby's lightweight floral nightgown could have been the nightdress of a princess. Her unbound red curls cascaded around them. Her knight in shining armor held her safely in the circle of his arms.

Yeah, Mrs. McClosky was going to have one heck of a story to tell in the morning, but Abby had a feeling she would have a better one.

Except she wasn't going to share it, not now, not ever. Maybe not even with her friends the Brewster women. This happy ending was the kind of story you kept in your heart.

* * * * *

#1 *New York Times* bestselling author

NORA ROBERTS

brings you more of the loyal and loving,
tempestuous and tantalizing Stanislaski family.

Coming in February 2001

The Stanislaski Sisters

Natasha and Rachel

Though raised in the Old World traditions of their
family, fiery Natasha Stanislaski and cool, classy
Rachel Stanislaski are ready for a *new* world of love....

*And also available in February 2001 from
Silhouette Special Edition, the newest book in the
heartwarming Stanislaski saga*

CONSIDERING KATE

Natasha and Spencer Kimball's daughter Kate turns her
back on old dreams and returns to her hometown, where
she finds the *man* of her dreams.

Available at your favorite retail outlet.

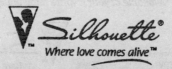

Where love comes alive™

Look Who's Celebrating Our 20th Anniversary:

"In 1980, Silhouette gave a home to my first book and became my family. Happy 20th Anniversary! And may we celebrate twenty more."

—*New York Times* bestselling author
Nora Roberts

"Congratulations, Silhouette, for twenty years of satisfying, innovative, rich romance reading. And hopefully twenty—or many more—years to come."

—International bestselling author
Joan Hohl

"In changing the world of romance publishing, Silhouette changed my life, both as a writer and as a reader. I'll always be grateful for their guidance, their teaching…and for the wonderful friendships that have grown from our long association."

—International bestselling author
Dixie Browning

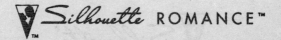

Silhouette ROMANCE™

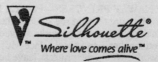

SILHOUETTE *Romance*

COMING NEXT MONTH

#1492 BE MY BRIDE?—Karen Rose Smith

Lauren MacMillan had never forgotten sexy Cody Granger. Then he returned to town, proposing a marriage of convenience to keep custody of his little girl. Dare Lauren trust Cody with the heart he had broken once before?

#1493 THE MESMERIZING MR. CARLYLE—Arlene James
An Older Man

He'd swept into her life, a handsome, charming, *wealthy* seafarer. But struggling single gal Amber Presley had no time for romance, though the mesmerizing Mr. Reece Carlyle seemed determined to make her his woman. Then she learned his secret motives....

#1494 TEX'S EXASPERATING HEIRESS—Carolyn Zane
The Brubaker Brides

She'd inherited a pig! And Charlotte Beauchamp hadn't a clue how to tame her beastly charge. Luckily, behaviorist Tex Brubaker sprang to her rescue. But his ultimate price wasn't something Charlotte was sure she could pay....

#1495 SECRET INGREDIENT: LOVE—Teresa Southwick

Businessman Alex Marchetti needed a chef, but was reluctant to hire beautiful and talented Fran Carlino. They'd both been hurt before in love, but their chemistry was undeniable. Could a confirmed bachelor and a marriage-shy lady find love and happiness together?

#1496 JUST ONE KISS—Carla Cassidy

Private investigator Jack Coffey claimed he was not looking for a family, but when he collided with little Nathaniel, he found one! As single mother Marissa Criswell nursed the dashing and surly man back onto his feet, she looked beyond his brooding exterior and tempted him to give her just one kiss....

#1497 THE RUNAWAY PRINCESS—Patricia Forsythe

Princess Alexis of Inbourg thought she'd found the perfect escape from her matchmaking father. But once she arrived in Sleepy River, she realized rancher—and boss!—Jace McTaggart was from a very different world. Would the princess leave her castle for a new realm—one in Jace's arms...?